After Fifth Grade, the World!

CLAUDIA MILLS

AN AVON CAMELOT BOOK

For Christopher

AVON BOOKS
A division of
The Hearst Corporation
1350 Avenue of the Americas
New York, New York 10019

First Avon Camelot Printing: January 1991

CAMELOT TRADEMARK REG. U.S. PAT. OFF. AND IN OTHER COUNTRIES, MARCA REGISTRADA, HECHO EN U.S.A.

Printed in the U.S.A.

OPM   10   9   8   7   6   5

ONE

"Four cents," Heidi Ahlenslager told her mother sternly. She pointed to the number displayed on the brand-new pocket calculator her parents had bought her for tomorrow, the first day of fifth grade. "I've double-checked all the subtractions, and your checkbook still says you have four cents more than the bank statement says."

Her mother laughed. "I'd say I'm making progress, then. Last month I was off by thirty dollars, wasn't I?"

"Thirty-seven fifty. You subtracted the phone bill twice." Heidi selected one of the freshly sharpened pencils laid out on the kitchen table like surgical instruments. "Now I have to go through all the checks from last month and make sure you wrote down the right amount for each one. I bet one of them's off by four cents."

"I'd leave well enough alone, honey, and not worry about balancing the account down to the penny. Four cents either way doesn't matter."

"It most certainly does matter," Heidi said. She

couldn't imagine giving up with four cents unaccounted for. "Besides, you want to learn from your mistakes, don't you?"

"Not particularly," her mother said. "And we don't know that it wasn't the bank's mistake. Banks do make mistakes sometimes."

"Yes, but you make mistakes, well, all the time. I wouldn't say it if it weren't—"

"True," her mother finished for her ruefully. "But only when I do the checkbook. In fifteen years of writing features for the newspaper, I've never had a mistake in one of my pieces. I have my first college journalism teacher to thank for that. He told us we'd get an automatic F for the entire semester if we had a single factual error in any of our work—even one misspelled name."

"He sounds mean," Heidi said, half-listening as she flipped through the stack of canceled checks one last time.

"Not mean, just strict. Though I guess I thought he was mean at the time. But I lived."

"Here, I found it! The check for Daddy's tropical fish. You wrote down forty-five forty instead of forty-five forty-four."

"My daughter, the checkbook wizard."

Heidi jumped up from her chair and gave a deep bow. "When I'm a world-famous accountant, I'll still do your checkbook for you for free."

"Are there any famous accountants?" Her mother sounded doubtful.

"You know those guys who add up the votes for the Academy Awards and put the winners' names in the sealed envelopes? Well, they're accountants. A billion people watch the Academy Awards every year, and someday that'll be me up there on TV, holding on tight to my locked briefcase with all the envelopes inside. H. P. Ahlenslager, president of the Price Waterhouse accounting firm."

Heidi liked to call herself by her initials. It made her sound tough and authoritative, a girl who wouldn't stand for any nonsense.

"And don't worry, Mom," she added graciously. "In my thank-you speech I'll name you and Daddy first for letting me practice on your checkbook."

"I hate to break this to you, Heidi, but the Price Waterhouse accountants don't get to make a thank-you speech."

"They will when I'm president. When I'm in charge, a lot of things are going to be done differently."

"First comes fifth grade," her mother said. She laid her checkbook on top of the microwave and wiped Heidi's cookie crumbs from the kitchen table. "Do you feel ready for school to start again?"

"I guess so. I mean, how ready do you have to be? You just go there, and it happens. Lynette's worried, though. She's heard that Mrs. Richardson is the meanest teacher in Hazlewood School."

"You're not worried?"

"Nah. She has more to worry about than we do. Twenty-five kids are a match for one mean teacher any day. Especially when one of them is H. P. Ahlenslager."

"Now, you don't *know* that she's mean. That's just a rumor, just hearsay, isn't it?"

"Oh, she's mean, all right," Heidi predicted calmly. "Where there's smoke, there's fire."

"But I think you should give her a chance before you make up your mind about her."

"Okay," Heidi promised. She took a handful of clean silverware out of the dishwasher and began setting the table for dinner. After all, even if they knew that Mrs. Richardson was mean, they didn't know *how* mean.

—————

Heidi's best friend, Lynette Lambert, rang the Ahlenslagers' doorbell at seven-thirty the next morning. Lynette was wearing a crisp, new red plaid dress that made her look like a model in a back-to-school fashion ad. Heidi had on clean jeans and a green batik T-shirt. She would have worn her T-shirt that said, "Kiss me, I'm an accountant," but it was in the laundry hamper. Lynette's blond curls were tied back by

4

a red plaid ribbon that matched her dress. Heidi's short brown hair, as always, was straight as straw.

Heidi and Lynette were opposite in other ways, too. Lynette wanted to be an opera star, and Heidi, though she shared Lynette's love of music, couldn't carry a tune. Math was Heidi's best subject and Lynette's worst. But the two girls had been friends since kindergarten and walked to school together every day.

"I've heard more horrible things about Mrs. Richardson," Lynette said as they headed off toward Hazlewood School.

"Like?"

"Like, you know how some teachers have pets? Well, Mrs. Richardson has *reverse* pets. She has kids that she hates for no reason at all, and she singles them out to pick on all year long."

"She won't pick on us," Heidi reassured her. "She'll pick on Skip and David."

"That's not all," Lynette said darkly. "Remember how Miss Bellini let us put on plays last year and brought in cupcakes for everyone's birthday? Well, in Mrs. Richardson's class, there are *no* plays, *no* cupcakes. Just work, work, work, every minute of the day."

From down the street Heidi heard boys' voices, singing. The song was low and mournful, like a funeral dirge.

"It's Skip and David," Lynette said.

Heidi listened harder. "Cheer up, Class 5C, the worst is yet to come!" they were singing. Class 5C was Mrs. Richardson's class.

The boys caught up with them. Red-haired David Wiggins, half a head taller than Skip Weinfeld, was wearing a black T-shirt and black pants.

"You look like you're going to a funeral," Lynette said.

"I am. Mine. Yours, too. Don't you have Richardson?"

Lynette glanced at Heidi, as if to say, *The evidence mounts.*

Heidi shrugged. "I'm not afraid of Richardson."

"Famous last words," David said. "Custer before his last stand: 'I'm not afraid of Indians.'"

"Tom Turkey before the first Thanksgiving," Skip chimed in. "'I'm not afraid of Pilgrims.'"

"I'm not," Heidi insisted.

David grinned at her. "My brother's guppy before the cat swallowed him: 'I'm not afraid of—'"

"Gulp," Skip finished ominously. Both boys smacked their lips with gusto.

The fifth graders were gathering on the far side of the blacktop outside Hazlewood School. Since the sixth graders went to Kennedy Middle School, Heidi and her friends were now the biggest kids in Hazlewood. Heidi could remember how wise and tall and ancient the fifth graders had seemed when she was in the lower grades. Now she was a mighty fifth grader herself. She wondered if the kindergarteners would bow and tremble when she walked by.

Lynette must have been thinking the same thing. "I always thought that when I was in fifth grade I wouldn't be afraid of anything. But having Richardson makes it feel like the first day of kindergarten all over again."

The bell rang. Heidi and Lynette took their places in the line for Room 5C, and the hall monitor led the class, single file, up one flight of stairs to the right-hand classroom at the end of the hall. Mrs. Richardson was waiting for them there.

Heidi couldn't tell if Mrs. Richardson looked mean or not. Tall, the teacher drew herself up even taller, as if an imaginary dictionary were balanced on her head. Heidi guessed that Mrs. Richardson was in her early fifties, but her hair was black without a smudge of gray. Not a strand was out of place.

Mrs. Richardson didn't scowl at the class, but she didn't smile, either. She surveyed them impassively, and it was impossible to know what she was thinking.

The children took their seats with none of the usual scrambling and commotion. Something about the set of Mrs. Richardson's head carried the message, *Don't even think about misbehaving.*

Then Mrs. Richardson smiled. "Welcome to fifth grade," she said.

Heidi found herself liking Richardson so far. When H. P. Ahlenslager was president of Price Waterhouse, she, too, would be thought stern and aloof at first. But once the junior accountants showed that they could do the job to her satisfaction, they would be rewarded by one of her rare smiles.

As Mrs. Richardson began making seat assignments, Heidi practiced this coveted smile of hard-won approval.

"Is anything the matter, Heidi?" Mrs. Richardson asked, motioning Heidi to the first seat in the first row.

The H. P. Ahlenslager smile disappeared abruptly. "No, Mrs. Richardson." There clearly wasn't much that Mrs. Richardson missed.

From years of alphabetical seating charts, Heidi was used to her front-row seat, halfway across the room from Lynette. Skip Weinfeld and David Wiggins were always placed next to each other at the back of the room, and they were always the first to have their seat assignments changed. The fourth-grade teacher had had to separate Skip and David before lunch on the first day.

"These will be your seat assignments for the entire year," Mrs. Richardson said. "I assume you can all behave where you have been seated."

Heidi didn't hear a peep from Skip and David.

"Very well, then. Let me give you the list of what school supplies you'll be needing."

Heidi glanced in her desk at her neat stack of yellow legal pads and big box of pencils. She had stocked up on school supplies last week.

"This year, all your assignments will be done on *white* lined paper," Mrs. Richardson went on. "Not yellow paper. Not green paper. Not pink paper. In fifth grade we take a serious, professional attitude toward our schoolwork, and this is reflected in the materials we use."

Mrs. Richardson glanced around the room for a telltale glimpse of the forbidden colors. Her eyes alighted on the thick tablet of bright pink paper set smack in the middle of Lynette's desk.

"Lynette, would you hold up your pad, please?"

Blushing furiously, Lynette obeyed.

"This, class, is the kind of paper I will *not* accept. I suppose it's fine for writing love notes"—from the back of the room someone snickered—"but not for doing serious schoolwork."

Heidi felt a surge of rage. How was Lynette supposed to have known that Richardson didn't like pink paper? It wasn't fair to make an example of her. And what was so unprofessional about colored paper, anyway? Heidi's father said that colored paper reduced eyestrain.

"All of your assignments this year will be done in *black* ink," Mrs. Richardson went on. She held up an old-fashioned-looking pen. "This is a cartridge pen, and it's the kind of pen I'll expect you to use. I know cartridge pens are more difficult to write with, but I'm a firm believer that by disciplining your hand, you discipline your mind, as well. Taking a few extra pains with your work won't hurt you at all. After the first week, ballpoint pen or pencil will not be acceptable. Make a note of this so you can tell your parents."

Heidi had never heard of anything more ridiculous. How could you do math with a cartridge pen? Heidi always did math with a freshly sharpened number 2 pencil. But she wrote it down, anyway, since Richardson was obviously watching to make sure everyone did.

"Lynette, since you were so kind as to show us your pad, would you now show us your pen?"

Heidi couldn't believe Richardson was picking on Lynette again. She twisted around in her seat to see the offending pen. It was Lynette's favorite, with a tiny, furry panda bear stuck on the end.

Lynette sat motionless, a spot of red burning in each cheek. Mrs. Richardson strode over to her desk. "May I?"

The teacher took Lynette's pen from her and held it high, for all to see. "For kindergarten, yes," Mrs. Richardson said. "For fifth grade, no. Thank you, Lynette." She laid the pen back on Lynette's desk. Lynette didn't pick it up again.

Heidi was sorry that she had liked Mrs. Richardson for even a fleeting minute. So what if Lynette used pink paper and panda-bear pens? That was her business, not Mrs. Richardson's, and the teacher had no right to make fun of her in front of the whole class. Mrs. Richardson was as mean as everyone had said. And she had made a very dumb mistake. She was going to find out that she couldn't pick on H. P. Ahlenslager's best friend without picking a fight with H. P. Ahlenslager herself. Mrs. Richardson was going to find out what it was like to have H. P. Ahlenslager as her sworn foe.

TWO

"We have to *do* something," Heidi said at the girls' table during lunch. She unwrapped her bologna sandwich and took a big, angry bite.

"She's already given us more homework today than Miss Bellini gave in a week," David grumbled from the next table.

"I don't mind the homework," said Pam Sorenson, who always got A's in everything. "But I'd die if Richardson picked on me the way she did on you, Lynette."

Lynette chewed intently on the straw from her carton of apple juice, as if she hadn't heard what Pam said.

"We could shoot her," Skip volunteered. "I know a song all about it, too." He cleared his throat and began to sing:

> "Ta-ra-ra boom-dee-ay!
> We have no school today!
> Our teacher went away.
> We shot her yesterday.

"We threw her in the bay.
She scared the sharks away.
Ta-ra-ra boom-dee-ay!
We have no school today!"

The others laughed appreciatively, but Heidi felt impatient. "We can't shoot her and you know it. It's against the law."

"*She* should be against the law," David said. "It should be against the law for a teacher to make you go out and buy a special pen. What's a cartridge pen, anyway?"

"You have to buy the ink yourself and put it in," Pam explained. "It comes in little plastic tubes—that's what a cartridge is—and if you don't put the cartridge in just right, it leaks all over the place. The ink is really wet and smeary, too."

David groaned. "I can tell you right now that my mom isn't going to want to buy me one. Not after I already made her buy me this combination ballpoint pen and water pistol. See, you write with one end and you squirt your friends with the other."

To demonstrate, he sent a fine mist of spray across the aisle to the girls' table.

"David Wiggins," the lunch monitor called out. "Any more of that and you can go see Mrs. Oberlin." Mrs. Oberlin was the principal.

"Maybe there *is* a law," Heidi said, still thinking. "There have to be laws about what a teacher can do."

"They can't hit you," Pam said. "If a teacher hits you, you can get her fired."

"So maybe she'll hit one of us," Skip said hopefully.

"Forget it," David said. "They never do."

They all finished their lunch glumly. June seemed an eternity away.

In the afternoon, Mrs. Richardson didn't pick on anyone else the way she had picked on Lynette in the morning. But she gave out even more homework and refused to let anyone get a drink of water after gym.

"We can't spend all afternoon traipsing to the water fountain," Mrs. Richardson said. "Concentrate on your math dittos instead, and you won't be thirsty."

"As if you can pick whether to be thirsty or not," Heidi said to Lynette as they walked back to Heidi's house together after school.

"I told you she was mean," Lynette said, without any gleeful satisfaction in having been proved right. Ever since the morning's incident, Lynette had been silent and subdued. She had hardly said a word at lunch.

"Listen," Heidi said, to console her, "we'll tell our parents and *they'll* do something."

Lynette stared at Heidi blankly. "Are you kidding? I'm not telling my parents that Mrs. Richardson yelled at me. They wouldn't understand, not in a million years. My mother's gotten involved in a new

14

project at her interior design company, and she's busy all the time now. She told me that she's counting on me to be a big help this year. The last thing she needs is for me to have problems at school."

"Well, I'll tell mine, then, and they'll come up with something," Heidi promised. "Wait and see."

The girls' parents had arranged for them to spend afternoons together, one week at Heidi's house and the next week at Lynette's, except on Thursdays, when Lynette had her piano lesson. That way neither one would have to be alone in an empty house while her parents were at work. Since both Heidi and Lynette were only children, this made them the next-best thing to sisters.

Heidi was glad that this was the week for her house. She sometimes wished that her parents kept their house tidy like the Lamberts. Her mother's checkbook wasn't the only thing out of order at the Ahlenslagers': Both Matt and Christy Ahlenslager were incorrigible packrats, living happily amid chaos and clutter. But at Heidi's house the girls could put their feet up on the coffee table or leave a half-assembled, thousand-piece jigsaw puzzle on the dining room table for weeks on end. At Lynette's they had to leave the house as neat and clean as they found it. And Lynette's mother always left strict instructions for snacks, but at Heidi's house they could invent whatever treat they wanted out of the groceries at hand.

As soon as they reached home, Heidi sent Lynette

to forage in the fridge while she called her mother to report that they were safely back from school.

"So how was it?" her mother wanted to know.

"We have to use cartridge pens! And white lined paper only! And she wouldn't let us get drinks after gym! And she picked on Lynette! And I have a ton of homework! And—"

"Honey, I have a deadline in fifteen minutes. But I want to hear all about it at dinner. Okay?"

"Okay. Bye, Mom."

Heidi replaced the receiver, disappointed. She had hoped her mother would say, *Stay right there! I'm on my way home, and when I get there we'll think of a plan of action.*

Lynette emerged from the kitchen with a bag of potato chips and a bowl of dip. "I made it from sour cream and Lipton onion soup mix. Is it any good?"

Heidi stuck her finger in the dip and licked it. "You should be a chef," she pronounced, "a world-famous chef."

"The recipe is right on the Lipton soup package," Lynette said. She followed Heidi down the hall to her room and plopped herself listlessly on Heidi's bed. "Don't you think we'd better get started on some of that homework? I don't know how we're going to get all those math problems done by tomorrow."

Heidi groaned good-naturedly. Actually, she could do math homework from dawn to dusk and never mind. She opened her math book to the first chapter, trying not to look too eager. The book had a wonderful, yeasty smell to it of fresh printer's ink on glossy new paper.

"Why don't we play a record?" she suggested. Maybe music would help Lynette cheer up.

Lynette searched through the stack of albums next to Heidi's record player, and in a moment the opening strains of the overture to *H.M.S. Pinafore* filled the room. Both girls loved Gilbert and Sullivan operettas. Lynette liked the soaring, warbling melodies, and Heidi liked the silly words.

Clasping her pencil tightly—they didn't have to use the dreaded cartridge pens for another week—Heidi began the homework problems. Seventy-five is what percent of three hundred? What is ninety percent of one hundred eighty? In spite of Mrs. Richardson, it was hard not to be happy in a world that had onion dip, *H.M.S. Pinafore*, and a brand-new math book in it. But then Heidi looked over at Lynette. Even humming along absentmindedly with "Oh Joy, Oh Rapture Unforeseen!" her friend looked miserable.

Heidi knew that Lynette still felt hurt and sore inside from the humiliating scene that morning, and remembering it, she hated Mrs. Richardson all over again. She wished the teacher had picked on her instead: She could take being picked on so much better than Lynette could. Lynette always took it so hard when a grown-up found any fault with her, but Heidi bounced right back. H. P. Ahlenslager wouldn't care if someone laughed at her for having a panda-bear pen.

She felt like telling Lynette, *Don't mind that old meanie*. But she thought that bringing it up would only make Lynette feel worse. Since Lynette herself hadn't said anything about it, it was better to act as if nothing had happened.

"This dip is scrump-dillyiscious," Heidi said, scooping the last of it onto the last broken potato chip.

"It's okay," was all Lynette said.

———

Lynette stayed till five-thirty. Heidi's father came home ten minutes later. Matt Ahlenslager was a research scientist for a big drug company. He invented new kinds of medicines.

"Did you find a cure for the common cold today?" Heidi called out in greeting. It was the same question she asked him every day.

Heidi's father kicked off his shoes by the front door, hung his tie on the doorknob, and tossed his briefcase onto the living room couch. Then he gave his daughter a bear hug. Heidi's father was a lot like a bear himself, solidly muscular and furry. Heidi nuzzled her face against his soft brown beard.

"How was school?"

"We have to use cartridge pens! And white lined paper only! And she wouldn't let us get drinks after gym! And she picked on Lynette! And I have a ton of homework! And—"

"It sounds like a typical first day of school, all right." Matt headed for the kitchen. "Your mother didn't happen to mention anything about dinner when you talked to her, did she?"

"It *wasn't* a typical first day of school," Heidi protested, watching as her father surveyed the contents of the refrigerator. "Richardson's different from other teachers. She's mean, really mean."

"How about beef stroganoff?" her father asked her. "I'll chop the onions if you'll wash the mushrooms."

Heidi emptied a pound bag of mushrooms into the colander. "Miss Bellini wasn't mean. Neither was Mr. Hsu. Or any of my other teachers."

"I seem to remember that you did your share of complaining those years, too."

Complaining! Of course she had complained. Complaining was just something you did, like eating or sleeping or breathing.

As Heidi ran water over the mushrooms, she told her father about Lynette's pink paper and panda-bear pen.

"That does sound mean," he admitted.

Heidi waited for him to promise that he'd go see Mrs. Richardson right away and tell her to leave Lynette alone.

"Well, I guess you kids are going to have to make the best of it," he said. "Hey, where's the sour cream? We can't make stroganoff without sour cream."

Heidi began searching the refrigerator shelves. Then she remembered. "We ate it. Lynette made onion dip. To go with our potato chips."

Her father laughed. "And I bet you're still hungry. Okay, how about spaghetti?"

By the time Heidi's mother walked in the door, the spaghetti sauce was simmering.

"Something smells good," she said. She draped her jacket on the back of the rocker, laid her purse on the coffee table, and abandoned her shoes in the middle of the living room rug. "Can I help?"

"We'll let you load the dishwasher," Matt said, kissing her after she had kissed Heidi. Lynette could never get over all the kissing that went on at the Ahlenslagers'.

At dinner Heidi told her stories over again, this time for her mother's benefit. But her mother didn't seem any more alarmed than her father had, or any more willing to leap into action on the children's behalf.

"Maybe things'll be better tomorrow," Christy Ahlenslager said. "Why don't you give it a couple of weeks and see how you feel then."

"If it's still awful then, will you guys go and talk to her?"

Heidi's parents exchanged glances. "If it's still awful then, we'll go talk to her," Matt said.

THREE

Give it a couple of weeks, Heidi's parents had said.
Heidi had to admit that was fair. In the back of one
of her notebooks she began keeping a list of bad things
and good things about fifth grade. To her surprise,
while the bad things side of the page was definitely
long and getting longer, the good things side had more
entries than she would have predicted on the first day.

For instance, math. Mrs. Richardson was, quite
plainly, the best math teacher Heidi had ever had.
Mrs. Richardson *liked* math. She taught it with evident gusto. All of Heidi's past teachers had seemed
resigned to teaching math. They taught it because it
was part of the curriculum, but they always had a
doleful tone in their voices as they announced, "Time
for math." Heidi had heard Miss Bellini confess to
Lynette that math had been her worst subject back
when she was in school. Miss Bellini, like Heidi's
mother, probably could have used some help with her
checkbook.

Mrs. Richardson knew amazing, astonishing facts about numbers. She told the class a secret shortcut for finding out whether any number was divisible by 3: You added up the individual digits of the number, and if that sum was divisible by 3, the original number was, too. So 249 could be divided by 3, because 2 plus 4 plus 9 equaled 15, and 15 was divisible by 3. The trick worked for every number, large or small. The sheer magic of it thrilled Heidi.

Math wasn't the only passion Mrs. Richardson shared with Heidi. The fifth-grade teacher was also wild about maps. Her classroom walls were covered with maps: maps of how the world used to look before Columbus discovered America, of Europe in the time of Charlemagne, of the United States in 1840. Best of all was a huge bas-relief map of the Western Hemisphere with the mountains sticking up in raised bumps, a long ridge of them stretching from Alaska down to the tip of Chile. Heidi had always loved maps; if she didn't become a world-famous accountant, she was going to be a world-famous mapmaker. In her room at home she hung maps she had traced out of the encyclopedia and her masterpiece—a full-scale map she had made all by herself of the Ahlenslagers' neighborhood. Heidi liked to know where she *was*. Gazing at the walls of Room 5C, she felt safe and secure, unlikely to find herself in Afghanistan or Budapest by mistake.

Most surprising of all, Mrs. Richardson read aloud to the class every day, before the final bell. She was reading *Johnny Tremain*, and somehow during those fifteen minutes the middle-aged teacher with her unsmiling face and glossy black hairdo seemed to *become* fourteen-year-old Johnny, a cocky silversmith's apprentice in Revolutionary War Boston. Heidi was so enthralled with Johnny's adventures that she almost checked the book out of the library so she could read ahead to find out what was going to happen. But that would be sort of like cheating, so she didn't.

If math, maps, and *Johnny Tremain* had been all of fifth grade, Heidi would have been perfectly happy. But on the other side of Heidi's list, the bad things side, was the inescapable fact of Mrs. Richardson's meanness.

She was so sarcastic! Heidi had once come across the phrase "withering sarcasm," and now she understood what it meant. Mrs. Richardson's sarcasm made its victim wither up inside, like a tender young plant scorched in the desert sun.

One day Denise Eisley, who sat in back of Heidi, had to confess that she didn't have her math homework to hand in. "I left my notebook at home," she explained.

Most teachers would have been content to tell Denise to bring it in tomorrow, marking the assignment down a grade for being late. But Mrs. Richardson peered at Denise over the top of her steel-rimmed half-glasses. "You're a big, husky girl," Mrs. Richardson said. "It shouldn't tax you too much to carry one thin little notebook."

And then poor, plump Denise had flushed scarlet, because everyone knew from Husky Boy clothing ads that *husky* was just another way of saying *fat*.

Sometimes Mrs. Richardson's sarcasm was funny. When she caught Skip in the lunch line struggling to balance his Ronald McDonald lunch box on his head, she remarked dryly that she was glad Skip had finally found *something* to use his head for. But usually the sarcasm wasn't funny, at least not to the person it was targeted against.

"Lynette," Mrs. Richardson said one morning the first week, after Lynette had given a hopelessly confused answer to a question in math, "maybe you'd have a better grasp of fractions if you spent more time on math and less time on your fingernails." Lynette hurriedly hid her hands beneath her desk, but not before the whole class had caught a glimpse of her perfectly manicured, pink-polished fingernails, with a tiny appliqué in the shape of a rose pasted neatly on each one. It had taken Lynette two hours to do her nails that time, Heidi knew, but Lynette also worked harder on math than anyone. The fingernails weren't the reason that Lynette got flustered in class when Richardson asked her a math question. At lunch that day Lynette went to the girls' room with the bottle of nail polish remover she kept in her desk. Five minutes later the beautiful roses were gone, and the pink fingernails, too. But even with unpolished fingernails, Lynette still didn't understand how to find a least common denominator.

The worst day was the day the class had to report to school with their cartridge pens.

"Does everyone have his or her cartridge pen?" Mrs. Richardson asked, right after the flag salute. "Hold up your pens so I can see them."

Every hand went up, holding a brand-new cartridge pen, except one.

"David Wiggins," Mrs. Richardson boomed, "did I or did I not make it perfectly clear that each of you was to bring a cartridge pen to school today?"

"Yes, I mean, you did, but—" David stopped.

"But what?"

"My mom wouldn't buy me one."

"Did you explain to her that this was a requirement for fifth grade?"

"She said I already had a pen."

Mrs. Richardson strode down the aisle and pounced on David's combination ballpoint pen–water pistol. "This is not a pen, this is a toy, and a ridiculous, infantile toy at that. Today you can sit quietly while the others do their work, since, having no pen, you are unable to participate. Tonight I will call your mother and see if I can do better at explaining the situation."

"You don't have to call her," David said, obviously panic-stricken. Heidi guessed that he had never gotten around to broaching the pen topic with his parents. "They'll get me the pen now, I promise."

"Very well," Mrs. Richardson said, returning to the front of the room, David's pen still in hand.

"Um—can I have my pen back?"

"In June," Mrs. Richardson said. She put the pen in her top desk drawer and then locked the drawer with a flourish. "Now, class, open your math books and do the first ten problems on page twenty-eight."

From the first stroke of her new cartridge pen, Heidi hated it. On the coarse-grained surface of her lined paper, the ink refused to make a neat, smooth line and blurred at the edges. Heidi gazed at her first, feathery equation in disgust. Math didn't look right written with a cartridge pen. She gritted her teeth and tackled the second problem. If even math was going to be spoiled for her, fifth grade was going to be bleak indeed.

Suddenly, from a row behind, Heidi heard a little scream. She turned around to see Lynette's face, ashen with distress.

"It's my pen," Lynette gasped, in answer to Mrs. Richardson's stern look. "It leaks!"

Sure enough, an enormous blot of black ink had

splashed onto Lynette's neatly written math paper. She held up an inky hand and, almost in tears, pointed to a great black stain on the cuff of her new pale pink blouse.

"Come, come," Mrs. Richardson said. "You're a big girl, Lynette, and crying isn't going to make things any better. Bring your pen here, and we'll see what the problem is."

As Lynette carried her wounded pen to the teacher's desk, Heidi could see a second ink splatter on the front of Lynette's matching pink skirt. In a few minutes Mrs. Richardson had the pen in working order, with the cartridge screwed in properly.

"You shouldn't have any problems now," Mrs. Richardson said. "Go wash up at the sink. If you apply yourself, you can have your assignment copied in time to hand in with the others."

Lynette retreated to the sink at the back of the room, but a first, quick rinsing did nothing to remove the ink. At lunch, Heidi joined Lynette in the girls' room, and the two girls did their best to give the stains a good scrubbing with soap and water.

"They won't come out!" Lynette's voice rose frantically. "Look, Heidi, they're as bad as ever."

"Your mom'll know how to do it. There's probably a special kind of cleaning stuff just for cartridge pen ink."

"I'm not telling my mother." Lynette's voice rose even higher. "I can't let her know that I ruined a

27

brand-new outfit after all the time she spent shopping for it."

"But it wasn't your fault. She's not going to be mad at you when it wasn't your fault."

"I hate school," Lynette said, and she was crying now. "I hate every single thing about it."

It was the week for Lynette's house, and Heidi and Lynette walked there soberly after school. Lynette held her books clasped in front of her so no one could see the stain on her skirt. All their scrubbing had, if anything, made the stain even bigger, as the ink bled into the surrounding fabric.

Once home, Lynette ran to change her clothes, emerging from her bedroom in a lavender pants outfit. "I put my pink skirt and blouse in the back of my closet," she said. "Way in the back, behind all my winter things. Do you think, since I have so many other clothes, that my mom won't notice I'm not wearing these anymore and she'll never have to find out about today?"

"Maybe," Heidi said. She still couldn't believe that Lynette's mother would punish her for something that was an accident. In fact, it was hard to imagine Lynette's mother punishing anyone for anything. She wasn't the punishing type. Heidi's parents, for all their friendly kidding, were perfectly ready to curtail TV or other privileges if Heidi didn't do as she was told. Once they had caught her making trick phone calls and had taken away TV for a month. But

Lynette's parents never even yelled at her, as far as Heidi could tell. In all the time she had been friends with Lynette, she had never heard them raise their voices.

"What would your mom do if she found out?" Heidi asked.

"I don't know," Lynette said. "But it's like she's under all this pressure at work, and she's busy all the time, and then she comes home, and I've made even more problems for her. I don't think she likes her job very much, and if I cause problems too, it's like one more thing she has to deal with."

Heidi didn't know what to say. It seemed to her that Lynette was making a big problem out of a little mishap. For Lynette it was the end of the world if anyone was unhappy with her.

The girls filed into the kitchen and found their snacks laid out for them on the table, an apple and two chocolate chip cookies apiece.

Heidi took a bite of her first cookie. "My parents said to give Mrs. Richardson a chance, to wait a couple of weeks and see if she turned out to be as awful as we thought the first day. It'll be one week tomorrow. What do you think? On a scale of one to ten, where one is perfectly nice and a hundred is as mean as can be, how mean is Mrs. Richardson?"

"That's easy," Lynette said. "A thousand four hundred and sixty-two."

FOUR

"You promised," Heidi told her father two weeks later, as her parents were getting dressed for parents' Back-to-School Night at Hazlewood School.

"I don't remember *promising*, exactly," Matt said. "Have you seen my tie?"

"It's in the kitchen. On the rack with the dish-towels." She followed him there. "You did, too, promise. You said that if it was still awful after a couple of weeks, you'd go talk to her. And it's been more than a couple of weeks, and it's still awful, so—tonight's the night!"

"Didn't I say that we'd *think* about talking to her?" Matt collected his tie from the towel rack and draped it around his neck.

"I wish I had a tape recorder. Mom! Didn't Daddy say—didn't he *promise*—that you guys were definitely going to talk to Richardson?"

Heidi's mother came into the kitchen in her stocking feet.

"Your shoes are in the hall. Where I almost

tripped over them after dinner. Mom, tell Daddy he promised."

"You promised," Christy said to Matt. Then, to Heidi, "Promised what?"

"Mom! Don't you guys pay attention to anything? That you'd talk to Mrs. Richardson. Tonight, at Back-to-School Night."

Suddenly Heidi's mother seemed to focus. "Oh, honey, I'm not sure that's a good idea. Teachers can't stand parents who interfere. And not tonight, when she'll have so many parents to deal with."

"Whose side are you on, anyway?"

"Yours, darling. I'm just saying that I'm not sure that talking to her is going to accomplish anything. It could backfire, you know, and make things even worse."

"So what are we supposed to do? Nothing?"

"Nothing does have a certain appeal, I have to admit," Matt said, checking his reflection in the door of the microwave to make sure his tie was straight.

"But you *promised*." Heidi clung fast to her opening point.

Her father sighed. "What do you want us to say?"

"She shouldn't pick on Lynette. She shouldn't be so sarcastic. She shouldn't make us use cartridge pens."

"Don't you think the business about Lynette would come better from Lynette's parents?" Christy asked. "They'll be there tonight, too, you know."

31

Yes, but Lynette never tells them anything, Heidi could have said. Instead she maintained a stubborn silence.

"And I don't see how we can tell her to curb the sarcasm," Christy went on. "What's perceived as sarcastic is so subjective. I'd hate to accuse her when we weren't on the scene to judge for ourselves."

"Cartridge pens," Heidi said. There was no way her parents could wriggle out of that one.

"I suppose we could say something about the pens," Christy conceded. "At least ask her about it. That does seem an idiotic requirement."

Heidi trailed her mother into the hall, where Christy's shoes stood waiting for her. "You won't forget?"

"We'll do our best. But don't expect too much, okay, honey?"

Heidi kissed her mother good-bye and gave her father a parting hug. Richardson couldn't fail to listen to *parents*. The dread cartridge pen days were numbered!

Exhausted from her lobbying campaign, Heidi felt like throwing herself onto the living room couch and killing a few hundred brain cells with a nice, numbing hour of TV. She could start with "Wheel of Fortune." But the couch, unfortunately, was uninhabitable, buried under several days' newspapers, Christy's tattered bathrobe, and back issues of Matt's pharmaceutical journals. The remote control for the TV had vanished a week ago, hidden somewhere amid all the clutter.

It was a sad state of affairs when a person couldn't even watch "Wheel of Fortune" in comfort in her own home. Heidi stalked over to the TV, turned it on by hand, and sprawled on the living room rug. Math assignments done in smeary cartridge pen. Lynette miserable at school. The living room couch turned into a junk heap. It had been a long time since Heidi had been so discouraged. And it was all so needless. There was no reason why everybody in Room 5C should have to use a cartridge pen, or Lynette should be afraid to talk to her mother, or Heidi's parents should live like slobs. Yes, that was the only word for them: slobs.

Well, Heidi had sent her parents off to banish the cartridge pens. She wasn't sure what could be done about Lynette, but before too long she'd think of something. And as for the mess. . . .

Heidi hopped up from the floor, ignoring the happy squeals and anguished groans of the "Wheel of Fortune" contestants. She began with the newspapers, and in twenty minutes she had them stacked, sorted, and stuffed into grocery bags for recycling. All her father would have to do was carry them out to the curb in the morning for the city's once-a-week pickup. Next Heidi gathered her father's journals and carried them upstairs to his overflowing study. *That* was a disaster area, but beyond Heidi's energies at present.

Back in the living room Heidi retrieved her mother's bathrobe and hung it in her closet. Four pairs of her mother's shoes were marched to their rightful home, lined up in a neat row under her parents' (unmade) king-size bed.

Finally Heidi rummaged under the cushions of the living room couch. She felt like an archaeologist excavating the ruins of Pompeii. There, as Heidi had suspected, lay the remote control for the TV, as well as her mother's extra set of car keys. She collected three dollars and forty-seven cents' worth of loose change, together with countless rubber bands and paper clips. She was just replacing the couch cushions when she heard her parents at the front door.

On seeing the living room, Matt did a double-take. "Excuse me, this must be the wrong house," he said, and turned as if to leave again.

"Daddy!"

"Heidi, is that you? Then this *is* our house. But something's different. The couch. Did you have it reupholstered? I don't remember its being blue."

"Daddy! You couldn't tell *what* color it was before because you couldn't *see* it."

Christy put her arm around Heidi and dropped a kiss on the top of her head. "You've done wonders, honey. I don't think I realized quite how messy it was. But now we could have this room photographed for the cover of *House Beautiful*."

"Or at least *House Much Neater*," Matt said. "It's

too bad we didn't take a 'before' picture, for contrast."

"I did it to celebrate," Heidi said, suddenly remembering the momentous mission on which she had sent her parents.

"To celebrate?" Christy asked, puzzled.

"No more cartridge pens!"

But one look at her parents' faces told her that something had gone wrong.

"You didn't tell her, did you? But you promised!"

"Hold your horses, Heidi," Matt said. "We did our darndest, your mother and I, but that woman's impossible."

"No kidding," Heidi said glumly. She had been so sure that her parents would come home triumphant.

Her mother put on water for tea, while her father dished up bowls of chocolate ice cream. Chocolate was the Ahlenslager family's favorite flavor.

"Okay, tell me about it," Heidi said, when they were settled back in the living room and the tea had been poured from her mother's pretty rose-patterned teapot. "Give it to me straight. I can take it."

"Well, I have to admit we thought you might be exaggerating just a wee, tiny bit, Heidi," Matt said, "but, whew! I'm glad I'm not a kid anymore."

"She talked about cartridge pens for half the time," Christy said. "I couldn't believe it."

"*And* the importance of white lined paper," Matt added. "Not yellow, not blue, not pink."

"I could see the sarcasm, too. According to Mrs. Richardson, kids today can't write, can't do math, know nothing about science or geography. She practically came right out and said that it was all the fault of parents." Christy took a slow sip of tea. "But there's something magnificent about her, don't you think?"

"Magnificent?" Matt asked. "Maybe in a ghoulish sort of way."

"It's that she really believes in something," Christy went on. "She really believes that everyone should grow up knowing math and geography. Teaching isn't a job for her, it's a mission. I mean, she really believes in those dumb cartridge pens."

"So what happened?" Heidi asked. "What did you say?"

"Well, after she had gone on about them for a while, I timidly poked up my hand. You've got to give me credit for courage, if nothing else, Heidi," her mother said. "And I asked, didn't she think that the choice of a pen was a personal matter best left to each individual? And I think I said that I couldn't see exactly why she thought it was so important."

Matt chuckled. "You said a bit more than that, as I remember. You used the words *petty* and *tyrannical*."

"Way to go, Mom! And what did she say?"

"She stared at me straight in the eyes, and she said, 'Mrs. Ahlenslager'—we had to wear nametags, so she knew who was who—'Mrs. Ahlenslager, I happen to believe in discipline. *Self-discipline*. And that's what the use of cartridge pens teaches.' Then she changed the subject, and that was that. So you can see that we tried, Heidi. But I could have told you— I did tell you, didn't I?—that it wasn't going to do any good."

Heidi licked her ice cream spoon with grim determination. All right, her first plan hadn't worked, but she would think of others, and if they didn't work, she'd keep on thinking until she found one that did. Mrs. Richardson hadn't heard the last yet from H. P. Ahlenslager.

Even though her mother's effort hadn't produced any concession from Mrs. Richardson on the cartridge pen issue, Heidi couldn't help bragging about it on the playground the next morning before school. "So then my mom said that everybody should get to pick what pen to use, that picking your own pen was a personal and private thing. She said it was a God-given inalienable right."

"Like in the Declaration of Independence," David said, obviously impressed. "Life, liberty, the pursuit of happiness, and picking your own pen."

"Right," Heidi said. The part about the God-given inalienable right hadn't been exactly what her mother had said, but Heidi knew it was what she had meant. "And then she said—get this!—that it was stupid and petty to make us use cartridge pens, well, petty at least. I know she said it was petty. And *then* she called Mrs. Richardson a tyrant—"

"She didn't," Pam interrupted, aghast.

"She did, too. My father said she used the word *tyrannical*. And that's like calling Richardson a tyrant, right to her face."

"All I can say is, you're lucky Mrs. Richardson didn't know whose mother it was," Pam said.

"Sure, she did. All the parents were wearing nametags. She knew."

"Well, then I feel sorry for you." Pam didn't sound very sorry at all. "Mrs. Richardson's going to know you put your mother up to it, and she's not going to be mad at your mom, she's going to be mad at *you*."

"It's a free country, isn't it?" Heidi said, with more bravado than she felt. "My mom can say whatever she wants to."

"All I know is, I wouldn't want to be you, Heidi," Pam said. "I wouldn't be you today for anything in the world."

The bell rang, and Heidi took her place in line.

"Don't listen to her," Lynette whispered. "She's just jealous because your mom is braver than hers." But despite her loyal words, Lynette looked as worried as Heidi was beginning to feel. Would Richardson bear a grudge against someone whose mother had called her a petty tyrant? She just might.

After the flag salute, Mrs. Richardson turned to the class. "I enjoyed meeting your parents last night," she said pleasantly. "The special requirements of fifth grade are as new to many of them as they are to you, and so it was helpful to be able to explain to them exactly what I expect and why I expect it. Apparently there has been some confusion over the requirement regarding the use of cartridge pens."

Heidi squirmed in her seat. She felt twenty-four pairs of eyes boring into her.

"But I think we've straightened it out," Mrs. Richardson went on. "I've been teaching fifth grade for thirty years, and for thirty years my students have managed to learn to write with cartridge pens. You will, too. I know it's difficult at first, but with discipline and perseverance, you'll be able to produce work you'll be proud of. If you were soldiers you wouldn't think to question your general's choice of weapons or ammunition, and as students I don't see any reason for you to question my teaching methods. Is that clear to all of you?"

Everyone nodded.

"Is that clear, Heidi?"

Heidi didn't say anything. For a fleeting moment she thought about leaping out of her chair and crying, "Number two pencils forever!" But maybe she'd be suspended, or expelled, if she said anything more. Heidi didn't want to be sent away from school for the rest of her life.

"I guess so," she said finally.

"Let's not have any guessing. Is it clear, or is it not?"

There was no help for it. "Yes," Heidi said, but behind her back she crossed her fingers, and in her heart was mutiny.

FIVE

On their way home from school, Heidi and Lynette stopped at the public library to get books for their science reports. Mrs. Richardson had assigned a report on a famous invention: who invented it, what technology it replaced, how it had changed the world. The report was due three weeks from Friday, but the topics had to be presented in class the next day.

For Heidi the science report was one more entry on her "Good Things About Fifth Grade" list. If she didn't become a world-famous accountant or a world-famous mapmaker, she might very well become a world-famous inventor. The only trouble was that most of the things she would have invented had already been invented by somebody else—like pocket calculators, electric can openers, and remote control devices for televisions.

When she was much younger, before the Ahlenslagers had bought their new TV, Heidi had told her parents, "Somebody should invent something so that you could turn the TV on and off and switch channels without getting up off the couch." She had been electrified by its possibilities: "Like, if a commercial came on, you could just go *click!* and switch to another station. And you could use it to make the volume louder or softer, too." She had been ready to rush right out and invent remote control, when her parents came home with a television set already equipped with all the miraculous capabilities she had envisioned. That had been a disappointment, although Heidi had been glad to have the use of the remote control sooner than she could have put the finishing touches on her invention.

Heidi still hadn't settled on the topic for her report. With every invention so interesting, it was difficult to choose. She was going to see how much information the library had on vacuum cleaners, microwave ovens, and electric popcorn poppers.

Lynette, on the other hand, didn't think any inventions were interesting. "The cotton gin," she said to Heidi, as they crossed the library parking lot. "You can't tell me that's not boring."

"Only because we've never seen a cotton gin, and we don't know very much about it. But, I mean, just think: Everything that ever was, was invented by someone. *Shoes* were invented. Shoe*laces*. Buttons. Paper clips. Somebody had to get up in the morning one day and say, 'Today I'm going to invent the paper clip.'"

Lynette giggled. "'Today I'm going to invent the toenail clipper.'"

There was no one Heidi could be as silly with as Lynette. "Today I'm going to invent the—door!"

"Today I'm going to invent the—doorknob!"

They were still laughing when they reached the library and walked down the curved staircase to the children's room. Skip and David were there, hauling books off the science and technology shelves.

"Have you picked your topics yet?" Heidi asked them.

"I have," Skip said, "but I can't tell. It's a secret." His shoulders shook with suppressed mirth. Apparently the very thought of his invention was hilarious.

"I can't decide," David said. "I'm either going to do the water pistol or the cartridge pen."

"You're not going to find anything on the water pistol," Lynette told him.

"Okay, then, the cartridge pen. I'm going to say it was the best invention ever and that all fifth graders everywhere should have to use it. Do you think she'll give me an A?"

"I think you should say it's the worst invention ever," Heidi said. She didn't think the cartridge pen requirement was anything to joke about, not after Lynette had ruined her skirt and Heidi had been humiliated in front of the whole class. "Why not be honest? But you're probably not brave enough."

"Are you kidding? Bravery is my middle name. David Bravery Wiggins. Sure, I'm brave. But I'm not suicidal."

"You aren't brave, either. None of you are. You all talk about Richardson, but you don't do anything." Heidi was surprised at how angry she was getting.

"What about you?" David asked. "What have you done?"

"I made my parents go talk to her."

"Big deal. It didn't do any good."

"That's not all I'm going to do."

"Oh, yeah? 'Yes, Mrs. Richardson. Yes, you're the boss, Mrs. Richardson.' You didn't sound very brave today."

"Just you wait," Heidi plunged on, stung by David's remarks. "I'm going to— Tomorrow, I'm going to go talk to Mrs. Oberlin!"

Heidi's reckless promise was received with a moment of awed silence. It was scary enough to be sent to the principal for punishment. Nobody ever marched into her den voluntarily.

"It was nice knowing you, Heidi," Skip said.

"You don't have to if you don't want to." Lynette glared at the boys.

"I do want to," Heidi said. "Come on, Lynette, we'd better start looking at some books on inventions."

Heidi flipped through the first few books mechanically. Discovering electromagnetism, inventing photography, laying the first transatlantic cable— what were these compared to a confrontation with the Hazlewood School principal? And what if Mrs. Ober-

44

lin told Mrs. Richardson about Heidi's visit? Heidi would be on Mrs. Richardson's most-hated list till the end of time.

But as Heidi began reading about Thomas Alva Edison, the Wizard of Menlo Park, her excitement at Edison's inventive genius made her forget her promise to David. "Listen," she said to Lynette. "This guy invented everything! It's like all the best, most famous inventions were all invented by the same person."

"He didn't invent the telephone," Lynette pointed out. "That was Alexander Graham Bell."

"Okay, but he invented the light bulb *and* the phonograph *and* movies. And the mimeograph machine: He invented *dittos*. It says here he had over a thousand patents."

"Let me see." Lynette leaned over Heidi's shoulder as Heidi traced her finger down the long list of Edison's inventions.

"I have an idea," Heidi said. "How about, I'll do my report on the light bulb, and you can do yours on the phonograph. You know, because you like music. That way we can share all the books. We could even make a club out of it. The Edison Fan Club. Or Future Inventors of America."

"I don't want to be an inventor," Lynette reminded Heidi patiently. "And I don't want to be in any club that has to do with inventions. But I'll do my report on the record player. It's better than the cotton gin."

"Or the doorknob," Heidi said, scooping up an armful of books to carry to the check-out desk.

"Or the cartridge pen," Lynette said, to carry on the joke.

The cartridge pen. In a rush, Heidi remembered her rash promise to talk to the principal tomorrow. If she could take it back, she would. But maybe, just maybe, talking to Mrs. Oberlin would solve everything. After all, Mrs. Oberlin was Mrs. Richardson's boss. She could boss her around if anybody could.

Heidi didn't have a chance to talk to David and Skip on the playground the next morning. But while in line to the school nurse to be weighed and measured, they both merrily pantomimed violent killings. Skip drew an imaginary knife across his throat. David pretended to strangle himself.

"When are you going to talk to her?" David mouthed the question.

"At lunch," Heidi mouthed back. She'd ask the lunchroom aide for permission to go.

Ten minutes before lunch, Mrs. Richardson announced that it was time to hear the science report topics. She positioned herself by the chalkboard to write down each topic as it was given.

"Heidi Ahlenslager."

"The light bulb."

"Marcia Brown."

"The telescope."

One by one, each student answered to the roll call. There was some duplication in topics—three kids had picked computers, four had picked television—but for the most part the inventions chosen made a diverse, wide-ranging list. Heidi would have liked to do a report on all of them.

Then came Skip's turn.

"Skip Weinfeld."

"The toilet."

A terrible hush fell over the room. Mrs. Richardson whirled around to fasten her hawk's gaze on Skip, but his look of blank innocence seemed to satisfy her. Turning back to the chalkboard, she wrote in her impeccably neat handwriting, "The toilet."

Heidi heard some low titters and a wave of muffled giggles. Then, to her horror, she heard a burst of hysterical laughter, laughter that sounded all too familiar.

"Lynette," Mrs. Richardson said icily, "would you care to share the joke with the rest of us?"

But the explosive power of laughter so long repressed could not be controlled. Poor Lynette was laughing too hard to answer and too hard to stop. Heidi barely restrained herself from joining in. *Today I'm going to invent the—toilet!* She forced herself not to look again at the list of inventions solemnly inscribed on the chalkboard.

Finally, Lynette's laughter subsided.

"I fail to see any humor in Skip's choice," Mrs. Richardson said once the room was quiet again. "Indoor plumbing has made an important contribution to our civilization, and I would hope that we would all be mature enough to study any notable invention, including the toilet."

Lynette shot a desperate look at Heidi, but she couldn't help herself: The word sent her off in another round of half laughter, half tears.

"Lynette! Since you cannot control yourself in class, you can go to the office and tell Mrs. Oberlin what you find so amusing. David Wiggins, your invention, please."

"The cartridge pen."

Without comment, Mrs. Richardson added it to the list. "Lynette, I thought I told you to go to the office," she said as Lynette sat motionless, crying now in earnest. Heidi had never felt angrier in her entire life.

At that moment, the bell rang. Lynette fled from the room, with Heidi in pursuit. Heidi caught up with her outside the school office.

She waited until Lynette had finished crying. "You need to blow your nose," she said. Lynette fumbled in her purse for a pack of pink-flowered tissues and blew her nose heartily.

"Oh, Heidi, I've never been sent to the office before. Never! It's so unfair. She should have sent Skip to the office, not me."

"Really," Heidi said. "Remember how he laughed yesterday when we asked him his topic? He picked it on purpose to crack everybody up, and then he just sat there, like, 'What's so funny?'"

"I can't tell Mrs. Oberlin what happened. I can't!"

"I'm going in with you. I told Skip and David I was going to go see her today, anyway."

"Are you sure?"

Before she could lose her nerve, Heidi took Lynette's sleeve and steered her into the outer suite of school offices. "Positive."

"May I help you, girls?" Mrs. Gates, the school secretary, asked.

"We're here to see Mrs. Oberlin," Heidi replied. "Mrs. Richardson sent us."

Mrs. Gates gave a gentle tap on Mrs. Oberlin's door.

"Come in!" the principal called.

Mrs. Gates pushed the door open partway. "Two girls from 5C are here to see you. All right, girls, you can go on in."

Heidi felt like Dorothy approaching the Wizard of Oz's inner sanctum as she stepped into Mrs. Oberlin's large, carpeted office. Certainly she felt more like Heidi, the Small and Meek, than H. P. Ahlenslager, the Great and Terrible.

But Mrs. Oberlin smiled at them kindly. She was a slim, dark-skinned woman, close to retirement age, dressed in a tailored gray suit with a plain blue blouse.

She gestured toward two comfortable-looking chairs facing her massive, oaken desk, and the girls sat down awkwardly.

"What seems to be the problem?" Mrs. Oberlin asked.

Heidi looked at Lynette, Lynette looked at Heidi, and then Heidi took a deep breath and started talking.

She told Mrs. Oberlin everything. If you're in for a dime, you're in for a dollar, her father said. At first she chose her words cautiously, but the serious, quiet attention with which the principal listened gave her courage to be bold. Cartridge pens, white lined paper, sarcasm, meanness, unfairness to Lynette—all tumbled out in a great torrent.

"Mrs. Richardson didn't send you in here to tell me all this, I presume," Mrs. Oberlin said when, at long last, Heidi had finished.

"No, she sent Lynette, because—well, for some other reason—and I came, too."

"Why did Mrs. Richardson send you, Lynette?"

"I laughed when I wasn't supposed to. We had to tell what invention we had picked for our science reports, and one boy said his, and I—laughed."

"What was his invention?"

Lynette hesitated. "The toilet."

A quick smile, unbidden, flickered over Mrs. Oberlin's grave countenance. Timidly, Lynette smiled, too. And then, all at once, the three of them were laughing—Lynette, Heidi, and the principal herself—almost as hard as Lynette had laughed before.

"Some things never change," Mrs. Oberlin said, wiping her eyes. "Who was the boy?"

"Skip Weinfeld."

"I could have guessed as much. All right, girls, we've had our laugh, and maybe we've all gotten it out of our systems. But your other complaints against Mrs. Richardson are more serious, and I'm going to tell you something that may surprise you. In many ways, I sympathize. Mrs. Richardson is very strict, maybe stricter than she needs to be, and I know she can be sarcastic. And, yes, many great thinkers and leaders have gone through life without ever writing with a cartridge pen.

"That said, now let me tell you this. Mrs. Richardson is here to stay at Hazlewood School. For one, she has tenure, which means, quite simply, that for all practical purposes she can't be fired. Period. And, for another, well, I wouldn't fire her if I could. I can promise you, as I've promised students before you—for this isn't the first time pupils have complained to me about Mrs. Richardson's methods—that Mrs. Richardson is one of those teachers whom you'll look back on in twenty years and say, 'I can't believe how much she taught me.' And teaching and learning is what school, in the end, is all about.

"I can tell you this, too. Mrs. Richardson has been teaching for thirty years, and she's not going to change. She's not going to adapt to you; you're going to have to adapt to her. And so, girls, my parting word to you is this: It's only September now, and June is a long way off. You're going to have to figure out how to get from here to there. But whatever you do, don't cheat yourselves out of the chance to learn as much as you can this year. You'll seldom have a better opportunity.

"Now, the two of you had better get some lunch." Mrs. Oberlin scribbled a hall pass on a scrap of paper and handed it to Heidi. "If you ever need to blow off some steam again, I'm here."

Out in the hall Heidi and Lynette, weak with relief, hugged each other.

"She's nice!" Lynette said.

"You can say that again."

But as the two girls raced down the hall to the cafeteria, Heidi couldn't help thinking that, nice as she was, Mrs. Oberlin hadn't turned out to be any more of a wizard than Oz himself. She had given them advice, but she hadn't changed anything. June seemed as far away as ever.

SIX

Toward the middle of October, Lynette's parents invited Heidi to go with them to a Friday-night performance of Gilbert and Sullivan's operetta *The Pirates of Penzance*. Heidi was to have dinner with the Lamberts before the show and sleep at their house afterward.

Heidi was thrilled at the invitation. She played her *Pirates of Penzance* record so often that her father warned her she might break it. (Heidi suspected he really meant that *he* might break it.) By Wednesday her small overnight bag was packed with clean clothes for the next day, a toothbrush, and her favorite pajamas.

On the way home from school Friday afternoon, the girls stopped at Heidi's house to pick up her suitcase.

"Do you realize that this is a historic occasion?" Heidi asked Lynette. "This is the first time that either of us has ever spent the night at the other one's house." Heidi's parents had extended a sleep-over invitation to Lynette several times, but her parents had always declined.

Lynette nodded. "My mother doesn't believe in sleep-overs. She says they make extra work and no one gets any sleep. But she made an exception this time because it's my birthday and we'll be getting back so late from *Pirates*."

She pointed to Heidi's suitcase. "Do you have everything?"

"Pajamas, clothes for tomorrow, toothbrush. That's it, I guess."

"You're not bringing a stuffed animal?" Lynette sounded mildly disapproving, as if every self-respecting traveler should have a teddy bear or two in her luggage. Lynette's own bedroom, by Heidi's estimate, contained more dolls and stuffed animals than most good-sized toy stores.

"No, but wait, I need my pocket calculator." Heidi took it from her knapsack and tucked it gently inside her suitcase. "In case we go to a restaurant and your father wants me to check the bill or figure out the right amount for a tip."

When they reached Lynette's house, Heidi wiped her feet with more care than usual. She felt oddly stiff and formal, on her best behavior.

"You're going to sleep in my room," Lynette said, leading the way upstairs. "I moved the animals from the bottom bunk of my bunk bed. But feel free to sleep with any of them you want," she offered generously.

Heidi set her suitcase neatly behind the door in Lynette's pink-flowered bedroom. Cleared of forty stuffed animals, the bottom bunk of the bed looked empty and bare, despite the pretty, pink gingham spread. The house was quiet, and for an awkward moment neither girl spoke. Then both started in at the same instant.

"Let's—"

"I—"

"You go first."

"*You* go first."

"Let's play records," Heidi said. "Let's play *The Pirates of Penzance*."

"That's what I was going to say!"

They raced downstairs, and in another minute the merry strains of the *Pirates* overture filled the family room. It was wonderful to think that in four more hours they'd be sitting side by side in the darkened theater, watching the pirate king himself bursting into song on the stage.

"Is there anything your mom wants us to do to help start dinner?" Heidi asked, once they had gobbled up the snack Mrs. Lambert had set out for them on the top shelf of the refrigerator: two small bowls of canned peaches, topped with crunchy granola.

"My mom doesn't like help in the kitchen," Lynette said.

"Why not?" The less Heidi's parents had to do in the kitchen, the happier they were.

"She says it's more trouble cleaning up after somebody else than doing it herself."

On the *Pirates* record, the chorus of singing policemen had begun one of Heidi's favorite songs, "The Policeman's Lot Is Not a Happy One."

"When the enterprising burglar's not a-burgling," Lynette sang along with the police chief.

"Not a-burgling." Heidi's flat alto joined in with the echo given by the rest of the musical police force.

"When the cut-throat isn't occupied with crime."

"'Pied with crime."

"He loves to hear the little brook a-gurgling."

"Brook a-gurgling."

"And listen to the merry village chime!"

"Village chime!" Heidi finished in her deepest growl. Yes, indeed, the record player was a wonderful invention.

"How far have you gotten on your report?" she asked.

"I haven't started it yet," Lynette said.

Heidi looked up, as surprised by Lynette's defiant tone as by the fact that her friend, always so punctual, had left her report to the last minute.

"But it's due next week."

"I know."

"If it's the topic— You don't have to do the phonograph just because of me."

"What does it matter what I do or when I do it, since Richardson will just pick on me, anyway?"

Heidi had never heard Lynette sound so bitter. She hardly knew what to say. "But you have to hand in *something*."

Lynette shrugged.

"Girls, I'm home!" It was Lynette's mother, calling down the basement stairs.

"We'll be right up," Lynette called back, and Heidi could tell she was glad for the interruption.

Mrs. Lambert was a tall, thin woman about ten years older than Heidi's parents. The Lamberts hadn't married until their late thirties, so they were older than most of the parents in Heidi's class. Lynette's mother was always meticulously dressed. She had her hair done every week and applied her makeup as carefully to go to the grocery store as to go to work or to the theater.

"Did you have a good day at school?" Mrs. Lambert asked the girls as she hung her jacket in the hall closet.

Heidi was about to launch into a typical story about Mrs. Richardson's meanness. That day she had sent Lynette to the chalkboard twice to do math problems that she knew perfectly well Lynette didn't understand how to do. But then she caught Lynette shaking her head slightly.

"It was fine," Lynette said.

"No problems with math?"

Lynette had stood miserably at the board while Mrs. Richardson had snapped at her, "Think, Lynette, *think*," as if you could simply command somebody to understand ratios.

"It was fine," Lynette said again.

Mrs. Lambert looked relieved. "You girls run along downstairs, and I'll start dinner. Unless you want to go ahead and get changed for the theater. We'll probably have to leave right after the birthday cake."

"I'm wearing what I have on," Heidi said cheerfully. "I wore a skirt to school today on purpose so I'd look right for tonight."

Mrs. Lambert took in Heidi's denim skirt and plain yellow shirt with what was clearly a pained glance, but she didn't say anything. Even if she had, it wouldn't have done any good. Heidi didn't own a single dress, and her only other skirt was as determinedly unfrilly as the one she had on.

Instead Mrs. Lambert turned to Lynette. "Why don't you wear your pink linen skirt and blouse outfit? You always look so pretty in it, and I don't think I've seen you wear it for a while."

Lynette shot one terrified look at Heidi. The pink skirt and blouse, stained with cartridge pen ink, were hidden in the deepest depths of her overcrowded closet.

Just tell her. Heidi tried to beam the message silently to Lynette.

"Well, I— You see, I thought I'd wear my new lavender dress, the one Aunt Muriel sent me. And maybe Daddy could take a picture of me wearing it, and I could send it to her with my thank-you note."

Lynette had recovered so gracefully from her first moment of panic that Heidi could only stare. She half admired her friend's coolness under pressure: She wouldn't have thought Lynette had it in her to deceive with such apparent ease and smoothness. But what would Lynette say the next time her mother asked about the ink-stained skirt? And the time after that? Heidi felt a knot in her stomach at the thought of being forced to continue day after day in such a drawn-out chain of interlocking lies. Besides, Heidi *knew* Lynette's mother. She wasn't a monster, just a perfectionist, like Lynette herself. Lynette was making life so much harder for herself than she had to.

Upstairs in Lynette's room, Heidi sat on the bottom bunk and watched Lynette begin the slow, luxurious process of preparing for the evening's grand event. She had never been able to figure out how anyone could take more than five minutes to get dressed—well, ten, if you had to take a shower first. But Lynette could devote five minutes to coaxing a single stray curl into place. She tried on four different pairs of earrings before deciding on the ones that looked best with her dress. But Heidi had to admit that Lynette looked beautiful when she was done. For good measure, she whipped out her own pocket comb and ran it once through her short, spiky hair.

The birthday dinner was more elegant than anything Heidi was used to at home, and delicious, too: salad, steak, baked potatoes, and broccoli with cheese sauce, followed by a cherry cake with pink frosting for Lynette's birthday.

Mr. Lambert was a short, stocky man who worked in a bank downtown. Heidi liked Lynette's father, partly because she could tell that he liked her. At least, he laughed uproariously at everything she said, whether she was trying to be funny or not. It was a standing joke between them that every time he saw her, he teased her again about the time she had been ready to reinvent remote control.

There was only one uncomfortable moment, just after they had finished the salad course. (Heidi's family never ate meals in courses.) Mr. Lambert, as always, asked Heidi what new inventions she was contemplating, and she found herself telling him as much as she could remember about Edison's astonishing achievements.

"So you're going to invent the light bulb, eh?" he asked, laughing, even though Heidi hadn't said any such thing. "What got you started reading about old Thomas Alva?"

"It's for our science report, Lynette's and mine. I'm doing the light bulb, and she's—"

Lynette's foot nudged Heidi's, hard, under the table, and Heidi broke off midsentence, confused.

"I didn't know you were working on a big project for school," Lynette's mother said. "When's it due?"

"We already handed it in," Lynette said quickly. "It wasn't that big, just a regular assignment."

Mrs. Lambert looked unsatisfied, but Mr. Lambert went on, chuckling, "You'll be inventing the wheel next, if I know you, Heidi."

Heidi didn't have a chance to talk to Lynette alone until they were about to leave for the performance.

"What did I say wrong, about the science project? Why did you lie?"

Lynette flushed. "If I told them they'd want to know how it's coming along, and it's not coming along. Nothing is coming along for me anymore. Everything is horrible."

"But they're going to find out sooner or later. When you get your report card—"

"But not today!" Lynette said fiercely. "Not on my birthday!"

And then Mr. Lambert came up behind them and announced that it was time to go.

The rest of the evening was pure magic. Seeing a live performance of *The Pirates of Penzance* was so vastly superior to hearing the record that Heidi wished she could see a Gilbert and Sullivan operetta every night. She clapped at the end of each act until her hands ached, and she left the theater with all her favorite songs singing themselves in her head.

"Someday that'll be you up on the stage," she told

Lynette. "*You'll* be Mabel, singing 'Poor Wandering One.'"

For answer, Lynette took up the song in her pure, soaring soprano, and to Heidi she sounded every bit as wonderful as the woman who had sung the role that night.

Back home, tucked snug and cozy into the bottom bunk of her best friend's bunk bed, Heidi thought she would drift off to sleep hearing again the rousing refrain sung by the pirate king and his men:

> *For I am a Pirate King!*
> *You are! Hurrah for our Pirate King!*
> *And it is, it is a glorious thing*
> *To be a Pirate King!*

But instead, for some reason, she kept hearing echoes of the evening's conversation.

> *"No problems with math?"*
> *"It was fine."*
> *"But they're going to find out sooner or later. When you get your report card—"*
> *"But not today! Not on my birthday!"*

SEVEN

By morning Heidi began to feel the first pangs of homesickness. It had been fun going to sleep in someone else's bed, but it would have been nice to wake up in her own. On weekend mornings at home she liked to tiptoe downstairs while her parents were still asleep and make the coffee. Heidi didn't drink coffee herself, but she loved filling the whole house with the wonderful aroma of it, and then hearing her parents' little grunts of appreciation when they stumbled into the kitchen for their first cup.

Up early at the Lamberts', Heidi felt like a prisoner of the bottom bunk bed. She heard Lynette's parents stirring in the kitchen, but she felt shy about drifting downstairs to join them. Mrs. Lambert had told the girls that breakfast would be at eight-thirty, and Heidi took that to mean that she shouldn't present herself in the kitchen any earlier. Lynette was still sound asleep—soft snores wafted down from the top bunk—so Heidi couldn't check with her on the best interpretation of the house rules.

Careful not to wake Lynette, Heidi reached stealthily for her pocket calculator, planning to while away the time till breakfast doing long division in her head and then checking it on the calculator. But in the hushed quiet of the room the clicking of the calculator keys sounded loud enough to wake the dead.

Heidi sighed and turned it off. Instead she lay very still in bed, thinking about school, and about Mrs. Richardson. By the time Lynette finally climbed down from the top bunk, Heidi had formulated a new plan.

Breakfast turned out to be as formal and elegant as dinner had been the night before. Mrs. Lambert served a fancy egg dish, garnished with a slice of orange and a sprig of parsley, just like in a restaurant.

Midmorning, Lynette walked Heidi halfway back to her house, and then Heidi ran the rest of the way. She could hardly wait to see her parents, to sprawl on her own bed, to smell the steaming pot of Ahlenslager coffee. Home!

Both her parents hugged her as if she had returned from a year in Antarctica rather than an overnight visit a few blocks away.

"There's no place like home. There's no place like home," Heidi said over and over again, like Dorothy come back at last to Kansas.

"You've grown!" her father said, standing back to squint at her.

"Have you eaten? Are you hungry?" her mother asked. "Daddy and I saved you some of our pizza from last night because we know you like it left over for breakfast."

"I'm stuffed. Mrs. Lambert made something called eggs Benedict Arnold."

"Eggs Benedict," Christy corrected. "Oo la la! So tell us all about it."

Heidi plopped down on the one clear corner of the couch—the results of her great tidying spree had long since been covered over with a new layer of clutter—and started in. She told them *almost* everything. She didn't feel right telling them how worried she was about Lynette. All she said was, "It's different there. Like, Lynette's parents don't really know about Mrs. Richardson. Lynette thinks they couldn't handle it or something. So they don't know half of what's going on. Or how we suffer."

Heidi was leading up to unveiling her new plan. The new plan depended on her mother, so Heidi chose her words carefully, watching for their effect on her audience.

"But I think they should know, don't you? I think everybody should know. Even parents whose kids don't have Richardson this year, because they might get her someday. And plain old citizens. They should know. They pay taxes, so they're the ones paying her salary, right? So they have a right to know what's going on in school."

Heidi waited a second, to see if her mother would go ahead and draw the obvious conclusion. But her parents just nodded in a noncommittal way. Apparently Heidi was going to have to spell it out for them.

"I think," she said, underlining every word, "that it should be in the newspaper. A big, front-page exposé on Mrs. Richardson, telling *everything*. No holds barred. The good, the bad, and the ugly. Mainly the bad and the ugly. Mrs. Oberlin says Mrs. Richardson can't be fired, but if there was this big newspaper story they'd have to fire her. The mayor would make them fire her."

Heidi's mother still didn't seem to see how any of this applied to her. It was time for Heidi to use her ace card.

"Plus, the person who wrote the article would probably get a Pulitzer Prize for investigative reporting. Imagine, Mom, a Pulitzer Prize for Christy Ahlenslager!"

"For me?" For the first time Christy showed some grasp of Heidi's point, but her face didn't light up with gladness at the thought of her impending Pulitzer. "Oh, honey, you think I'm going to write an article about your teacher for the *Herald*?"

"Page one," Heidi said. "Extra, extra, read all about it!"

"But, Heidi . . ." Christy looked imploringly at Matt. "A mean teacher isn't— I mean, there have been mean teachers since the beginning of time. Mean ones and wonderful ones and in-between ones. Every kid in America, I'd bet, gets at least one mean teacher at some point in school. A mean teacher is just a part of life. A mean teacher isn't *news*."

"Well, it should be!" Heidi couldn't believe that her own mother refused to understand. "There have been murders since the beginning of time, and you print stories on murders. There's probably a murder in the paper every single day."

"But a *murder* is much more serious than a mean teacher."

"Not to the kids who have one. Not to kids." Tears of disappointment formed a knotty lump in Heidi's throat.

"Look, Heidi, I'm sorry—"

"You should be! It serves you right not to get a Pulitzer Prize. You don't deserve a Pulitzer Prize!"

Matt reached over and rumpled Heidi's already rumpled hair. "I know this year is tough on you, but that's no reason for you to make things tough on your mother. Come on, chin up and cheer up."

Heidi scowled.

"Okay," Matt said. He stood and put on his jacket, which was conveniently draped over the closest stereo speaker. "Your mother and I have an hour's worth of errands to run, so that gives you an hour to sulk. Then when we get back, all cheerful people with their chins up can go out for tacos. Is that a deal?"

Heidi didn't answer.

"Your sulking time starts"—Matt consulted his watch—"now!"

He and Christy headed out the front door.

Ooooh! Heidi was furious. Her parents didn't understand about Mrs. Richardson any more than Lynette's parents did. They didn't understand anything. Heidi gave a savage kick to her father's galoshes, which for the past week and a half had stood patiently by the coffee table. Then, too angry to sit still, she retrieved first the right and then the left galosh from where her mighty kick had flung them, marched into her parents' room, and hurled the unfortunate galoshes into the depths of her father's closet. Her parents would be gone an hour, would they? Well, when they got back they'd find that some changes had been made.

In the living room last week's newspapers, as always, covered the couch. Grim and unsmiling, Heidi sorted and bagged them, and then dragged them to the curb. From the basement she brought up the large wicker laundry basket. Into it she tossed three pairs of Christy's shoes, two of Matt's ties, books, magazines, earrings, unopened junk mail, a lipstick, a flashlight, and a roll of wrapping paper. Then she stowed the laundry basket out of sight in the basement utility room, behind the furnace.

Her final step was to post, in a prominent place on the refrigerator door, the list of new house rules. She wrote them on a big piece of red construction paper with thick black Magic Marker.

AHLENSLAGER HOUSE RULES
by order of H. P. Ahlenslager

1. Leave newspapers in a neat pile on the coffee table after reading. Remember that others may want to read the paper after you. Newspapers are to be kept for one week's time in a stack behind the couch. Once a week Matt Ahlenslager will bag them up and carry them to the curb.

2. Each person's clothes belong in each person's own bedroom. Remember that you share this house with others, and that others may get the idea that items left lying around are trash and should be thrown away.

3. Ditto for other personal belongings.

AHLENSLAGER HOUSE MOTTO:
A place for everything,
and everything in its place.

Cheerful and with her chin up, Heidi reclined luxuriously on the cleared living room couch to await the arrival of her parents.

When Matt and Christy returned a few minutes later, they first took Heidi's burst of housecleaning to be a peace offering.

"Thank you, honey," Christy said, looking relieved at Heidi's evident change of temper. "I'm glad you understand our side of things a little bit."

Then they saw the list on the refrigerator. Matt gave a low whistle.

"So you're out to reform us, are you, Heidi? Who are these 'others' you keep talking about? Anybody we know?" He read through the list a second time. "If I didn't know better, I'd think that rule number two was some kind of veiled threat."

"A word to the wise is sufficient," Heidi said primly. It was one of Mrs. Richardson's favorite sayings.

"I know we could all stand to be a bit neater," Christy began.

Or at least two of us could, Heidi thought.

"But we don't want to be so—I don't know—critical of one another that we forget the things that make us a family, the things that are really important."

"Like what?" Heidi asked.

"Tacos," Matt said. "I'm starving. Let's go eat."

EIGHT

"I have an idea," Christy said, her second taco poised in midair. Matt and Heidi both had their mouths full of refried beans, ground beef, shredded lettuce, Monterey Jack cheese, and taco sauce, so she went on. "It's about your teacher, Heidi. Now, don't say it won't work until you've heard me out. What if, just once, you guys tried being extra nice to her?"

"It won't work," Matt and Heidi said automatically, as soon as they finished swallowing their enormous bites of taco.

"Why wouldn't it? Usually if someone's difficult to get along with, it's because that person has been hurt at some point in her life. Sarcasm and meanness are usually defense mechanisms. I don't see why you couldn't get around Mrs. Richardson's defense mechanisms by some unexpected act of kindness."

"Like what?" Heidi asked. She couldn't afford to dismiss any suggestion, however bizarre, without at least considering it.

"Give her a surprise party. I'm sure you could think of some sort of occasion for a party. Or everybody chip in and get her a present and a really nice card."

"Apples!" Matt said jovially. "Kids who like their teachers are supposed to bring them apples. So one day next week the whole class comes in with apples, an apple from every kid, twenty-five apples all lined up on Mrs. Richardson's desk. Twenty-five little arrows into her heart. She'll be a goner."

"You're teasing me," Christy said to Matt, "but I'm serious. You've heard the saying 'You can catch more flies with honey than you can with vinegar.' All that means is that niceness can pay off in the end. Okay, it sounds sentimental and corny, but my guess is that under that stern, cold exterior, Mrs. Richardson's got a heart as much as anybody else. Niceness is worth at least a try."

The big newspaper exposé had also been worth at least a try, but Heidi knew better than to reopen that discussion.

"Which do you think would be better?" she asked. "Apples or a party?"

"Apples," Matt said.

"A party," Christy said.

So Heidi found herself organizing an apple party in honor of the meanest teacher in Hazlewood School. She told the others about it before school on Monday morning.

"It won't work," Lynette said, just as Heidi had two days before. "Mrs. Richardson doesn't have a

heart, or if she does, it's made of stone. Stoneheart."
She savored the name with a melancholy satisfaction.
"That's what we should call her: Stoneheart."

"If I give her an apple, can I poison it first?" Skip
asked. "Or get one that looks red and shiny, but inside
there's a big, fat, juicy worm!"

"You know what she'll do with the apples, don't
you?" David chimed in. "She'll stick razor blades
in them and give them out to little kiddies on
Halloween."

"You boys are disgusting," Pam said. "I think
Heidi has a good idea. I think Mrs. Richardson would
love it if we gave her a party. Probably no one's ever
given a party for her in her whole life. Maybe she'll
even cry, and then the whole rest of the year she'll
be as sweet as can be."

"There'll be a cake," Heidi said. It was only fair
that her mother should have to bake them a cake,
since the party had been her idea in the first place.
"A chocolate layer cake with chocolate fudge
frosting."

Skip had heard all he needed to hear. "Then count
me in."

"Me, too," David said.

"Me three," said Pam.

"Lynette?" Heidi turned to her friend, hoping to
hear a grudging *Me four*.

"I already said what I think. But go ahead. Do
whatever you want. I don't care."

Heidi sighed. "Okay. I'll send around a note this morning to ask the others. And then we'll have to get busy making the rest of the plans."

Heidi knew better than to try to circulate a note under Mrs. Richardson's watchful eye. She waited for music class, at ten o'clock. Miss Vane, the music teacher, was young and good-natured. The only thing that mattered to Miss Vane was volume: If the class sang loudly and lustily enough, Miss Vane was willing to forgive any rustling papers or furtive whispers overheard between choruses. So Heidi sang with all her might, as her note passed down one aisle and up the next.

> "I've been working on the railroad
> All the livelong day.
> I've been working on the railroad
> Just to pass the time away. . . ."

Two songs later the note had come back to her, signed by all of Room 5C. Everyone wanted to go on record in favor of a chocolate layer cake with chocolate fudge frosting.

Heidi still felt there should be a *reason* for the party, a real reason, not a maybe-if-we're-nice-to-Mrs.-Richardson-she'll-be-nice-to-us kind of reason. If only it was Mrs. Richardson's birthday! Maybe if Heidi asked in the office, they'd tell her that Mrs. Richardson's birthday was the day after tomorrow, or Thursday, or Friday. It *might* be—it had to be some day. But maybe teachers' birthdays were kept top secret. And suppose they said, as seemed only likely, that Mrs. Richardson's birthday wasn't in October at all, but in February, or May, or August? With Heidi's luck, Mrs. Richardson's birthday would probably turn out to be on Leap Year's Day, like Frederick's in *Pirates of Penzance*, celebrated only once every four years.

"Look," Heidi said to Pam at lunch, "we need a reason for the party, don't you think? Like, it's Mrs. Richardson's birthday. Or it's National Teacher Appreciation Day."

"Well, is it? Either of those days?"

"No. I mean, I don't think so. It would be a pretty big coincidence if it was. Unless— Do you think we could just pretend it's National Teacher Appreciation Day? After all, I don't even know that there is such a thing. I just made it up now. If I'm making it up, I guess it can be on whatever day I make it up for."

"Don't worry about it," Pam advised. "She'll be so thrilled when she sees the cake, with her name on it in great big letters, that she won't care what day it is."

Heidi wasn't sure about that at all, but Pam said, "Trust me."

The party was set for Friday afternoon, and Thursday night Heidi's mother obligingly baked the cake. She made it in an enormous rectangular pan, big enough so there would be a generous piece for everyone. Across the thick fudge frosting spread on the top she wrote, in pale blue icing, "For our teacher, Mrs. Richardson." In each corner she made a pale blue icing rose. Actually, the roses looked more like pale blue icing blobs, and the lettering had a decided downhill slant to it. But having licked the cake batter bowl and both frosting bowls, Heidi could report that, whatever its flaws as a work of art, the cake was delicious.

Matt drove Heidi and Lynette to school on Friday morning. David and Skip were waiting for them, to help carry the party provisions: party plates, cups, and forks, two jugs of fruit punch, the cake in a huge cardboard box, and a sack filled with twenty-five ripe, red apples. Heidi had been afraid that Mrs. Richardson might notice their unusual packages and even ask to inspect them, but the children managed to get everything safely stored away in the back of the locker alcove without attracting any attention.

All morning long, the class fidgeted restlessly, impatient for the coming party. There were three cartridge pen accidents, which somewhat dampened Heidi's enthusiasm for National Teacher Appreciation Day.

"What is wrong with you children today?" Mrs. Richardson asked, as the third ink puddle was being wiped up with paper towels. "If you can't settle down, we'll skip our chapter of *Johnny Tremain* this afternoon and have a math quiz instead."

Someone giggled, for of course there would be no *Johnny Tremain or* math quiz, just satisfying slabs of chocolate layer cake with chocolate fudge frosting.

"That does it," Mrs. Richardson snapped. "A math quiz it is."

At lunch Heidi distributed the apples, remembering her father's vision of a polished apple on every desk. She was beginning to think the plan was positively brilliant. But she hoped that Mrs. Richardson didn't really cry when the moment of the party arrived. Heidi didn't like it when grown-ups cried. It was too embarrassing.

After lunch came science, and Mrs. Richardson collected the reports on inventions, which were due that day. Heidi had finished hers earlier in the week, and she was almost as excited about it as she was about the party. It was definitely the best report she had ever written. She imagined Mrs. Richardson reading it and exclaiming, "Why, the child is a second Edison!" She envied Mrs. Richardson the thrill of having such a talented student, who very well might have invented the light bulb herself if only she had lived a century ago and thought of it first.

Heidi hadn't asked Lynette anything more about the phonograph since the *Pirates of Penzance* sleep-over. She was relieved when Lynette laid a yellow-covered report in the pile with all the rest. Maybe at the last minute Lynette had fallen in love with the record player the way Heidi had fallen in love with the light bulb. At least she had come up with something. Last weekend Heidi had been afraid Lynette might boycott the assignment altogether.

With his report, Skip handed in a scale model of his chosen invention. A wave of giggles swept across the room as Mrs. Richardson set his foot-high replica of a flush toilet next to the pile of reports on her desk. Heidi turned around to glance at Lynette, but this time Lynette wasn't laughing.

Mrs. Richardson wasn't laughing, either.

"All right," she said. "Clear your desks, except for one piece of white lined paper and your cartridge pens. It's time for our math quiz."

What it was, was time for a party, but Mrs. Richardson didn't know that yet. All eyes were on Heidi as she raised her hand.

"Yes?" Mrs. Richardson asked impatiently.

"Um, before we have the quiz, well, there's something we want to give you."

"Can't it wait until three o'clock?"

"No. You'll see."

Heidi motioned to David and Skip, who followed her to the locker alcove, out of view of the rest of the classroom. She handed David the bag of party supplies, and Skip took the two jugs of fruit punch. Carefully Heidi lifted her mother's cake out of its box and took her place at the head of the procession. "One, two, three," she prompted, under her breath. "Go!"

Out into the room they marched.

Heidi had planned to set the cake in the middle of Mrs. Richardson's desk, but, with all their reports and Skip's flush toilet, there wasn't any room. So she stood holding it awkwardly, tilting it slightly so that Mrs. Richardson could read the inscription.

"Apples!" she mouthed at the class. On every desk an apple appeared.

Then she led the class in the prearranged cheer. "Two, four, six, eight! Who do we appreciate? Mrs. Richardson! Mrs. Richardson! Hooray!"

But halfway through the *Hooray!* she made the mistake of looking over at Mrs. Richardson to see if she was crying yet. The *Hooray!* died on Heidi's lips. Mrs. Richardson wasn't crying. Neither was she smiling.

"Would someone please tell me what this is all about?" Mrs. Richardson asked coldly, in the silence that hung in the air after the unfinished cheer.

Heidi knew that she was the someone Mrs. Richardson had in mind. "It's National Teacher Appreciation Day," she explained, by now almost believing that it was. "And we wanted to let you know that we, well, that we appreciate you." Even as she said it, that part sounded patently untrue to Heidi.

"Did you get permission from Mrs. Oberlin to have a party on school grounds during school hours?"

"No, but—" Who could possibly object to a National Teacher Appreciation Day party? Who could object to a chocolate layer cake with chocolate fudge frosting?

"Then I can't permit this to continue. Hazlewood School rules authorize three parties annually, for Halloween, Christmas, and Valentine's Day. All other parties require the prior permission of the principal. Presumably your parents send you here to learn something, not to waste your time on frivolity."

Heidi was still holding the cake. It was heavy, and her arms were beginning to ache. Mrs. Richardson hadn't even bothered to read the pale blue icing message written across the top.

"Now, if you'll take those things back to wherever you got them, we can get on with our math quiz."

David and Skip beat a hasty retreat to the locker alcove, but Heidi stood her ground.

"We were trying to be *nice*," she said, her voice trembling. "We were trying to show you that we like you. Don't you even care?"

"Frankly, I don't," Mrs. Richardson said, her steely gray eyes meeting Heidi's furious brown ones. "I've never cared about winning classroom popularity contests. I care how much my students learn."

Heidi glared at Mrs. Richardson. Mrs. Richardson glared back. But it was only a hollow victory for Heidi that the teacher looked away first.

NINE

One of the nicest things about Lynette as a best friend was that she never said "I told you so." Instead, as soon as the bell rang, she silently helped Heidi carry the party provisions out to the playground. David and Skip trailed behind.

"I hate her," Heidi said, the first to speak. She set the cake on the blacktop next to the swing set and dropped down wearily beside it. "I feel like taking this stupid cake and smashing it into a million pieces."

"Now, wait a minute!" Skip said, alarmed. "There's no reason why we can't have the party, anyway, the four of us. Look on the bright side. This way there's that much more cake for *us*."

"I'll cut the pieces with my Swiss Army knife," David offered. "You guys start pouring the punch."

"I'm not hungry," Lynette said.

"Me, neither." Anger always took a toll on Heidi's appetite. "Why don't you go ahead and have the party without us? You can keep the cake. The punch, too. Lynette and I are going home."

"Did you hear that, David?" Skip asked. "Make the pieces *really* big."

Heidi and Lynette exchanged a disgusted look. The others had never cared about the purpose behind the doomed party. Their concern had begun and ended with the chocolate layer cake.

It was the week for Heidi's house. By the time they reached home, Heidi's gloom had lifted enough for her to feel a twinge of regret that she had given the entire cake to Skip and David. It wasn't the cake's fault, after all, that Mrs. Richardson was such a party pooper. A thick slice of it would have made a very nice afternoon snack. But the instant chocolate pudding the girls whipped up in its stead also proved satisfactory.

While they waited for the pudding to set, Heidi called the *Herald* and broke the news to her mother that, as predicted, niceness had been an utter failure.

"At least we tried," Christy said.

Yes, and speaking of trying, how about that newspaper story? Heidi wanted to say. Instead she confessed, "I gave away the cake. I hope that's all right."

"It's the best news I've heard all day. Anyone who wants to gain five pounds is welcome to it. Sooner them than me."

When Heidi returned to the kitchen, she found Lynette reading the list posted on the refrigerator. "'A place for everything, and everything in its place,'" Lynette read aloud, laughing. "That doesn't sound like your house to me."

Heidi had to admit that at that moment the Ahlenslager kitchen failed to live up to the house motto. As usual, her mother's shoes stood smack in the middle of the floor. The headphones from her father's transistor radio dangled from the top of the toaster oven. A month-old copy of *Newsweek* was propped open on the cookbook stand. Evidence of the recent baking of a chocolate layer cake was everywhere, from the empty pan on the counter to the telltale drips of chocolate batter on the stove.

Grimly, Heidi disappeared down to the basement and returned with the same large laundry basket that still stored her parents' scattered clothes and books from the previous weekend. Into it she now tossed the shoes, the radio, and *Newsweek*. She debated including the cake pan, but decided against it. Then she made a quick roundup of the living room.

"Don't they get mad?" Lynette asked. "Don't they wonder where you've put all their stuff?"

"That's the pathetic part. They've hardly even noticed. My mother missed a pair of shoes the other day, and when I found them for her in the laundry basket, she thought I was a miracle worker. Besides, they have so much junk. My mother must have fifteen pairs of shoes. Who needs fifteen pairs of shoes?"

"Well . . ." Lynette shared Heidi's mother's fondness for pretty footwear.

"Okay, you have a lot of shoes, too. Some people like shoes. I can accept that." Heidi herself wore the same pair of scuffed sneakers every day, until it was cold enough that her mother made her wear boots. "But magazines? If my parents quit their jobs tomorrow and did nothing but read magazines all day long, they'd still be about three years behind. I mean it. Or ties. My father has never thrown away a tie in his life. Even if they're ugly, or he's spilled something on them, or he hates them, they're still somewhere in his closet.

"Or lawn mowers. My father has *three* old lawn mowers. When people put their broken-down lawn mowers out at the curb for the bulk trash pickup, what does my father do? He goes and brings them home with him, like they were some kind of great treasure. Or empty ice cream cartons. My parents *save* empty ice cream cartons. And let me tell you, they eat a *lot* of ice cream. Or olive jars—"

"I get the picture," Lynette interrupted hastily. "So are the rules working out? Are you getting them to change?"

"What do you think?" Heidi pointed to yet another pair of high-heeled pumps, peeking out from under the skirt of the living room couch. "Basically, they think the rules are a joke. Because, like, what am I going to do if they break them? Take away their allowance? Send them to bed early with no TV?"

Heidi lowered her voice. "But I've thought of something I can do, and I'm going to do it. When this basket gets full, when it gets really full, I'm going to call Good Will and their truck is going to come and

84

take it away. And maybe a couple of lawn mowers, too."

"You wouldn't!"

"I would. When the going gets tough, H. P. Ahlenslager gets going."

But even as she said it, she knew that all her toughness hadn't made any difference where she wanted to make a difference most, at school. Her parents' intervention hadn't worked. Talking to Mrs. Oberlin hadn't worked. Niceness hadn't worked. What was left to try?

Suddenly the answer was so obvious that Heidi couldn't believe she hadn't thought of it before.

"Meanness," she said to Lynette, swinging one of her mother's shoes by its thin leather strap. "We could give her a taste of her own medicine and be mean right back."

"To your mother?" Lynette asked, bewildered.

"To Mrs. Richardson. We could show her what it feels like to be made fun of in front of everybody. We could make fun of her in front of the whole school. Maybe at the big safety assembly next week."

"But— Heidi, I know I sound like a broken record, but it won't work. Remember what Mrs. Oberlin told us? She said that Mrs. Richardson's never going to change."

"Grown-ups always think everything's impossible. They told Columbus he'd never discover America, and they told Edison he'd never invent the light bulb, and they told the astronauts they'd never go to the moon. And what happened? Lots of 'impossible' things happened, that's what. I saw a bumper sticker on a car the other day, and this is what it said."

Heidi recited dramatically:

> "The difficult we do immediately.
> The impossible takes a little longer.
> Miracles by appointment only.

"We'll get Mrs. Richardson to change," she insisted. "It'll just take a little longer, that's all."

Lynette sighed. "We'll just get in trouble, that's all."

Heidi tossed her mother's shoe on top of the very full basket. One more clean-up session and she'd be ready to call Good Will. And she had the first stirrings of a perfect plan for teaching Mrs. Richardson what meanness was all about.

———

Heidi spent most of the weekend alone in her room, working on what she had decided to call Project Meanness. For it she needed a roll of brown wrapping paper, poster paints, and a picture of a witch in a pointed witch hat to use for a model.

She drew her picture first on a practice piece of paper, cut to the scale of her finished poster, but much smaller. Heidi had never considered being a world-famous artist, but she was used to taking pains with whatever she did, and her artwork for school generally turned out pretty well.

She knew she couldn't make the witch look exactly like Mrs. Richardson, so she placed her in front of a classroom door prominently labeled Room 5C. That should give people a first clue for the witch's true identity. Mrs. Richardson always wore a scarf knotted around her neck, held with a gold pin; so did Heidi's witch. Heidi's witch wore shoes like the ones Mrs. Richardson wore every day. And instead of a broom, Heidi's witch carried an enormous, menacing cartridge pen.

When it was finished, the sketch was so funny that Heidi was tempted to run downstairs to show it to her parents. But she had a feeling that they wouldn't approve of Project Meanness. Whatever their faults as housekeepers, her parents were both extremely nice people. And the whole point of Project Meanness, after all, was to be mean.

Was the poster *too* mean? For a moment Heidi hesitated. But then all the anger she had felt against Mrs. Richardson, from the very first day of school, flooded over her again. Mrs. Richardson shouldn't have made fun of Lynette for her pink paper, her panda-bear pen, or her slowness in math. She was responsible for the cartridge pen accident that had ruined Lynette's new outfit. She had made Lynette cry for laughing at Skip's invention. Enough was enough, and H. P. Ahlenslager had had enough some time ago. Besides, she reminded herself, they had already tried everything else. Project Meanness was all that was left.

It was a big job to copy the sketch onto a gigantic piece of brown wrapping paper and a bigger job to paint it in with the poster paints. Heidi toiled for hours, and still she wasn't done.

"My, you're working hard up there," Christy commented, when Heidi wandered downstairs for a break Saturday afternoon.

Heidi knew that was her mother's friendly way of inviting her to tell them about her project.

"I guess so," she said uneasily.

"You don't have to tell us what you're working on if you don't want to," Christy added. And then, of course, Heidi felt terrible for having a secret from her parents, especially a secret they wouldn't like. Maybe she'd tell them once Project Meanness had proven a great success.

Lynette came over on Sunday afternoon. When they were alone together in her room, Heidi got ready to unveil the finished poster.

"Close your eyes," she commanded. "Don't open them until I say *when*."

Lynette squinched her eyes shut.

Carefully Heidi unrolled the poster in the middle of the floor, weighting down each corner with a volume of the World Book Encyclopedia so it wouldn't roll back up again.

"When!"

Lynette took one look at Heidi's masterpiece and obligingly fell down on Heidi's bed, shrieking with laughter. "It's perfect! You drew her shoes!"

"And her scarf. You know, with the gold pin."

"And, oh, Heidi, the cartridge pen!"

Heidi gazed at her work with calm satisfaction. Lynette's reaction to it was highly gratifying.

"Do you think it needs a caption? Something like *The Wicked Witch of Room 5C*."

"How about *Stoneheart*?"

"That's it!" Heidi knelt down on the floor, pencil in hand, to figure out where the caption would fit.

"I wrote a song about her," Lynette volunteered. "About Stoneheart. Do you want to hear it?"

Heidi looked up expectantly. In her clear, sweet soprano, Lynette sang:

> "We hate our teacher, Stoneheart.
>   She is so very cruel.
>   We used to like to come here,
>   But now we just hate school."

The tune was so rousing that Heidi joined in off-key. The girls sang through five straight choruses of the Stoneheart anthem, louder on each one, until Matt yelled upstairs that he was trying to watch the football game and could the Metropolitan Opera please practice someplace else.

"But what are you going to do with the poster?

Where are you going to hang it?" Lynette asked then.

"Don't worry," Heidi assured her. "I have a plan for that, too."

———

On Monday, Heidi and Lynette taught the Stoneheart song to Skip and David, and by midweek the boys had taught it to the rest of the fifth grade. "We hate our teacher, Stoneheart," was warbled on the playground. It echoed at lunch tables. Snatches of it wafted up from the water fountain line. Lynette was accorded new respect as its author. "That's the girl who wrote the Stoneheart song," some fourth graders whispered when she walked by.

The poster, wrapped up nice and tight in an empty cardboard tube, was stowed safely in Heidi's locker during most of the week. On Thursday, the day of the schoolwide safety assembly, Heidi darted by her locker to get it and unobtrusively carried it down to the all-purpose room for lunch. When no one was looking, she hid it in the folds of the dusty red velvet curtain that hung at one end of the room.

Back in class, ten minutes before the assembly was to begin, she raised her hand and asked permission to get a drink of water.

"You can get one on the way to the assembly," Mrs. Richardson said. Mrs. Richardson would have refused a request for water from soldiers dying on a battlefield.

Heidi began coughing, as hard as she could without making the cough sound too fake.

"Oh, go ahead, then," Mrs. Richardson snapped.

Out the door Heidi flew. She was back in less than five minutes, her heart pounding so loudly she felt sure the whole class could hear it.

At two o'clock, Room 5C lined up to go down to the all-purpose room. As the biggest kids in the school, they joined the other fifth graders in the rows farthest back in the room and sat down cross-legged on the floor. The lower grades filed in after them.

Mr. Schwartz, one of the fourth-grade teachers, was in charge of AV. He was busy in the back of the room threading the safety film onto the school's ancient projector. Then he strode toward the front to set up the movie screen, four hundred pairs of eyes on him. But when he gave the rolled-up screen his practiced tug, there appeared not the usual blank white surface, but a funny brown-paper poster of a wicked witch who looked oddly like Mrs. Richardson, stapled in place by none other than the fearless, the dauntless, the intrepid H. P. Ahlenslager.

The little kids began laughing first, delighted by the occurrence of anything unexpected. Then one of the fourth graders called out, "It's Stoneheart!" The fifth graders of Room 5C gave a collective gasp of mingled horror and pleasure.

Mr. Schwartz, startled, snapped the screen shut again, but it was too late. The all-purpose room rocked with laughter, until Mrs. Oberlin herself stepped up to the microphone and called for order.

Heidi shivered at the magnitude of her success, beyond anything she could have hoped for. Beside her, Lynette was pale with shock at Heidi's daring, but laughing in the helpless, uncontrollable way she had laughed over Skip's invention.

Then Heidi felt a hand on her shoulder.

"Would you girls please step out into the hall? You, Heidi, and Lynette. I'd like a word with you."

It was Mrs. Richardson.

TEN

Heidi had always hated to watch adventure programs on television. The story lines of the programs were invariably the same: The hero was trapped in some terrible predicament, maybe in an abandoned mine shaft with the water rising, and time was running out. Would he manage to escape somehow, defying all the odds against him, or would he be killed so that all the rest of the shows in that TV series for the rest of the year would have to be canceled? He was never killed, of course. There was always a happy ending, but what drove Heidi crazy was the agony of waiting for it. If everything was going to turn out okay in the end, why not have it turn out okay *right now* and save her the suffering? She would stalk out of the room and go stand in the kitchen, her eyes fixed on the kitchen clock, counting off the minutes that would have to elapse before the hero was out of the mine shaft with the heroine clasped in his arms again.

So when Heidi followed Mrs. Richardson out into the hall, she felt a powerful desire to be in the kitchen at home, concentrating on the clock until the signal came from her parents that the worst was over. If only she could switch channels and watch "Wheel of Fortune" for the next ten minutes! By then Mrs. Richardson would have said whatever she was going to say, and H. P. Ahlenslager would have said whatever *she* was going to say, and Heidi's fate, whatever it was going to be, would have been decided.

Reluctantly she forced herself to pay attention to the gory, gruesome present.

"I suppose you two are feeling proud of yourselves right now," Mrs. Richardson said.

As a matter of fact, Heidi was feeling considerably less pleased and proud than she had expected to. Now that she was face to face with Mrs. Richardson, with Stoneheart herself, Project Meanness seemed quite a bit meaner than it had when she had planned it all alone in her room. But something else Mrs. Richardson said stopped her short: *you two.*

"It wasn't Lynette's fault," Heidi blurted out, aware that by denying any blame for Lynette she was tacitly admitting it for herself.

"Oh, no?" Mrs. Richardson asked coolly. "I believe Lynette has been exercising her musical talents lately in the field of song writing, has she not?"

Both girls said nothing. Lynette's fame as "the girl who wrote the Stoneheart song" had evidently spread a bit too far.

"As for you, Heidi, perhaps now you see why I'm reluctant to grant requests for unsupervised trips to

94

the water fountain. Perhaps now you see why I've learned not to assume that all students are trustworthy."

Heidi felt a twinge of shame. She looked down at her dirty sneakers.

"I cannot permit a school assembly to be disrupted in this way. Nor can I permit the teachers of Hazlewood School to be held up to public ridicule." No one who didn't know better would have guessed that Mrs. Richardson had been the teacher ridiculed. "Therefore, I must take disciplinary action of the most severe kind."

Heidi began counting off seconds in her head: one elephant, two elephants, three elephants . . . In five minutes, three hundred elephants, the worst part would have to be over.

"For the rest of the year, I'm revoking your privilege of attending school assemblies or participating in parties or field trips. When your classmates report to an assembly, you will report to Mrs. Oberlin's office. You can spend the classroom Halloween, Christmas, and Valentine's Day parties in her office, as well. In April, when we have our class trip to the state capitol, other arrangements will be made for both of you. Do you understand?"

Forty-one elephants, forty-two elephants . . . "Yes, Mrs. Richardson," Heidi remembered to say. It was increasingly hard to tune out the dismal reality that was unfolding. Heidi didn't care about missing assemblies, but she hated to think how disappointed Mrs. Oberlin would be in her two new friends when she heard Mrs. Richardson's side of the story.

"Of course I'll be calling your parents, also."

Heidi squirmed. Her parents would be disappointed in her, too. But then she caught a glimpse of Lynette's face. Lynette looked like a prisoner who had just heard her death sentence read aloud by the executioner.

Heidi would have been too proud to beg for herself, but she couldn't bear to see Lynette so frightened and miserable.

"Please, Mrs. Richardson, don't call Lynette's parents. Please! It was all my fault. It really, truly was."

"Maybe you girls should have thought of the consequences of your actions *before* you wrote songs and made posters."

"But you're not being fair. I did a hundred times more than Lynette did, and you're punishing us the same. No, you're punishing *her* a hundred times *more* because she minds having her parents called so much more than I do. Please, do anything you want to me— put me in jail, even—but don't call Lynette's parents."

"I'm afraid you're going to have to let my judgment on this be final," Mrs. Richardson said. "You may go now to Mrs. Oberlin's office for the rest of the assembly. I'll expect you back in class at a quarter to three."

With that, Mrs. Richardson turned on her heel and swept away.

Heidi expected Lynette to burst into tears, but she didn't. Silent and white faced, like a sleepwalker, Lynette started down the deserted hall to the principal's office. Heidi hurried after her. Should she say anything? What should she say?

"You know," she ventured, "I bet your parents won't mind as much as you think they will. I bet they'll be pretty understanding."

"If that's what you think," Lynette said, "then *you* don't understand *anything*."

After that, Heidi didn't say another word.

She was glad Mrs. Oberlin was still at the safety assembly. But Mrs. Gates, the school secretary, gave them a look of chagrined disapproval.

"You, again!" She shook her head. Any kid could be sent to the principal's office once, but if you were sent there twice, Mrs. Gates's pursed lips seemed to say, it was plain you were a hardened criminal. Certainly this time was a hundred times worse for Heidi than the last time had been.

At a quarter to three, Heidi and Lynette went back upstairs to Room 5C. Mrs. Richardson didn't take any notice of them as they slipped into their seats, but the rest of the class stared.

"I want you to take these home to show your parents," Mrs. Richardson was saying. Take what home? Then Heidi noticed the stack of folders in the middle of Mrs. Richardson's desk. Mrs. Richardson was about to return their science reports.

Proceeding in alphabetical order, Mrs. Richardson handed Heidi's report to her from the top of the pile. Heidi felt so dispirited that she almost stuffed it in her knapsack without looking at the grade. But with the report right in front of her, she couldn't resist turning to the last page to receive the verdict.

She gave a sigh of relief. At least one thing in her life had turned out right. At the very bottom of the page, Mrs. Richardson had written (with a cartridge pen, of course), "A+, a splendid job." Heidi couldn't have put it better herself.

She didn't dare ask Lynette how she had made out with the phonograph, and she didn't need to. As soon as they were outside, Lynette took her report from her knapsack and tore it into what looked like a hundred pieces. These she flung into the nearest dumpster without a backward look.

"How did *you* do?" Lynette asked then.

"I got a—B." It was the first time Heidi could ever remember telling a lie to Lynette.

"You did not," Lynette said wearily. "You got an A."

"Well, sort of." *A+, a splendid job*. "But, Lynette,

I mean, what happens now? What are you going to do?"

Lynette stopped walking and scuffed at the gravel with the toe of her perfectly polished black Mary Jane shoes. "My mom's home sick from work this afternoon, and I have my piano lesson. But I don't think Mrs. Richardson'll call till tonight, because she knows people work. And tonight I'm just going to make sure she doesn't get through. I'll secretly take the phone off the hook, so it'll be busy every single minute. Or maybe I'll break it or something."

"What if she tries to call again tomorrow?"

"Tomorrow I'll do the same thing. And the next day. And forever. Or I'll answer the phone myself and pretend I'm my mother. That's what I'll do. I'll make my voice deep, like this." Lynette said the last words in a low growl that made her sound a bit like a talking gorilla, but not at all like somebody's mother.

Heidi had never heard a more hopeless plan in her life. But Lynette sounded so desperate that she didn't know how to come right out and tell her, *Your plan stinks*.

"It might work," Heidi said doubtfully, since Lynette seemed to expect her to say something.

"It *has* to work!"

They parted a block from Heidi's house. Lynette headed off to her piano lesson, and Heidi hurried home to see if Good Will had made their pickup. In all the afternoon's misery, Heidi had almost forgotten that this was the day the Good Will van was scheduled to make its collection. When she had called them earlier in the week, they had told her to have any bundles out at the curb by 9 A.M. on Thursday. That morning, as soon as her parents had left for work, Heidi had hauled four huge cartons of junk down to the edge of the lawn, together with two of her father's three lawn mowers. She could easily have filled ten more cartons if she had had enough cartons and time.

When she came within sight of the house, Heidi saw that Good Will had indeed come and gone, taking the first satisfying shipment of trash and clutter with them. She had rescued her father's Sony Walkman from the laundry basket, and three or four pairs of her mother's shoes, but for the most part she hadn't weakened throughout the packing and bundling operation. After all, it was for her parents' own good.

Once inside, Heidi made herself a cheese sandwich and collapsed on the couch. Her science report grade and the Good Will pickup had helped somewhat to salvage the day, but it was still, on balance, the single worst day of her entire life. Project Meanness had failed, and failed utterly. The Stoneheart poster wasn't going to make Mrs. Richardson be any less mean. If anything, Heidi had to admit, it gave her an excuse to be even meaner. Heidi didn't like thinking about how Mrs. Richardson must have felt when the cruel caricature of her was displayed to the explosive laughter of the whole school. No, it wasn't any more fun, really, to be on the giving than on the receiving end of meanness.

Heidi's parents were going to be mad when Mrs. Richardson called them that evening. She could count on that. And Lynette's parents— Did Lynette really think she could solve anything by trying to hide her problems from her parents, telling them lies and more lies and lies on top of lies? Heidi felt worse about Lynette's excruciating burden of guilt and deception than about everything else put together. If she could make things right between Lynette and her mother, it wouldn't matter so much that she had failed with Mrs. Richardson. If Lynette couldn't talk to her mother, someone else would have to do the talking for her, and soon, very soon, before Mrs. Richardson picked up the phone. It was Lynette who was trapped in a mine shaft now, with the water fast rising, and time running out. Somebody had to save her, and Heidi knew all too well who that somebody was. It was H. P. Ahlenslager.

═══

In five minutes, Heidi had run the four blocks to Lynette's house and rung the bell. Mrs. Lambert, dressed in her stylish blue velour bathrobe, answered the door a moment later.

"Lynette's still at her piano lesson," Mrs. Lambert explained. She dabbed at her very red nose with a flowered tissue.

"I know." Heidi took a deep breath. "I didn't come to see Lynette. I came to see you."

"To see *me*?" Mrs. Lambert sounded flabbergasted. "But, Heidi, I have a terrible cold, as you can see."

"It's important."

"Well, come in, then. Can I offer you anything?"

"No, thank you." Heidi sat down on the edge of the couch, and Mrs. Lambert settled herself in the wing-back chair facing her. "You see," Heidi began, since she might as well say what she had to say and get it over with, "you see, it's about Lynette."

Once she had started, the rest was easy. Heidi told Mrs. Lambert everything, from how Mrs. Richardson had made fun of Lynette's pink paper and panda-bear pen on the first day of school through the unveiling of the Stoneheart poster and its disastrous aftermath. She told Mrs. Lambert that Mrs. Richardson picked on Lynette so much that Lynette didn't want to try in school any more. She told her about Lynette's science report, about the Stoneheart song, even about the ink-stained pink linen skirt and blouse hanging in the back of Lynette's closet.

Then she was done. She had said everything she had gone there to say.

Lynette's mother blew her nose violently. Her eyes were as red as her nose now, and Heidi prepared herself for the possibility that a grown-up was going to cry.

But Mrs. Lambert didn't cry. She blew her nose twice more, and then she asked, "But why didn't Lynette tell me?"

"Why didn't I tell you what?"

Lynette stood in the doorway, her sheaf of piano sheet music tucked under her arm.

"About Mrs. Richardson and the trouble you've been having in school." Mrs. Lambert sounded so angry that for the first time Heidi wondered if maybe, just maybe, she had made a big mistake. "We have a lot of talking to do."

Lynette stared at Heidi, then at her mother, then back to Heidi again.

"You told her!" she cried in a low, passionate voice. "How could you?"

Heidi felt taken aback. She had expected Lynette's eyes to light up with relief and gratitude that the weight of her dread secret had at last been lifted from her. But in her friend's face she read only an accusation of betrayal.

"I thought she should know," Heidi said.

"*You* thought! Who are *you* to have an opinion about what *my* mother should know?"

The answer seemed obvious to Heidi. "I'm your friend."

"No, you're not," Lynette said, her voice trembling with fury. "I thought you were, but I know now you're not my friend and you never were and you never will be."

"But, Lynette—" Mrs. Lambert began.

Heidi didn't wait to hear any more. The cruel finality of Lynette's words came close to breaking her heart. She jumped up from the couch and rushed blindly across the living room to the front door. Out in the street again, she raced toward home, swallowing back the lump in her throat.

She saw her father's car in the driveway and ran even faster. Her parents would understand that she had only been trying to help, to step in to work a miracle in Lynette's relationship with her mother. *The difficult we do immediately, the impossible takes a little longer, miracles by appointment only.*

Her father met her at the door. But just as Heidi was about to fling herself into his arms, she caught a glimpse of his face. Heidi couldn't believe it. He looked every bit as angry as Mrs. Richardson, Mrs. Lambert, and Lynette.

"Where are the lawn mowers?" he demanded in a sterner tone than Heidi had ever heard from him before. "And the books and magazines you've been collecting from the living room? And my ties and your mother's shoes? Mrs. Barnett next door tells me that she saw the Good Will truck here this morning, making quite a pickup. If that means what I think it means, you're in very deep trouble, Heidi Patricia. You're in the trouble of your life."

The trouble of her life was too much trouble at the end of a day that had included disaster and disgrace at school and the loss of Heidi's best and oldest, her closest and dearest friend.

"You don't understand!" she was surprised to hear herself shouting. "Nobody understands anything!"

And with that, H. P. Ahlenslager—future world-famous accountant, mapmaker, and inventor, ready to take on all tasks difficult, impossible, and miraculous—burst into tears.

ELEVEN

Upstairs in her room, Heidi didn't even bother to kick off her dirty sneakers before pulling down the covers and climbing into bed. She could hear her father on the telephone, calling Good Will to find out if he could reclaim any of Heidi's donations. A few stray phrases drifted up the stairs. "My ten-year-old daughter . . . acting without permission . . . of course, my wife and I are very angry. . . ." Heidi put a pillow over her head to block out the rest.

She had only wanted to help! But every single one of H. P. Ahlenslager's grand, sweeping projects had ended in unmitigated disaster. She had tried to change the world, and the world had refused to budge. No, it was worse than that. She had tried to change the world, and the world—at least the part of it that Heidi cared about most—had blown up right in her face.

She could hardly believe that everything had turned out so badly. They were all so angry at her: Mrs. Richardson, her father, Lynette. But no one could have tried any harder than Heidi had. Shouldn't she at least get an A for effort? Where would civilization be today if all the great thinkers, the movers and shakers, had been sent to their rooms every time they tried to make a few small improvements in the world around them? Edison had tried and failed hundreds of times before he found the right filament for his miraculous new light bulb. Wasn't H. P. Ahlenslager entitled to a failure or two of her own? Apparently not. Well, if all her trying only made everyone mad at her, she just wouldn't try anymore, that's all.

A deep, deadening sense of discouragement overwhelmed Heidi. She had been so sure that the world would thank her for all the magnificent and splendid light bulbs she was going to invent for them. But she knew in her heart that this time around she hadn't accomplished anything magnificent and splendid at all. She couldn't really blame the world for withholding its gratitude. The difficult had proved too difficult. The impossible was simply impossible. And H. P. Ahlenslager knew better now than to expect any miracles.

A knock came on Heidi's door.

"Come in," she called glumly.

It was her father. "You're in luck. Good Will said we can go down right now and get our stuff off their truck. So grab your jacket, and let's go."

Neither Matt nor Heidi spoke a word for the first few blocks of the ride downtown. Then Matt broke the silence.

"What's gotten into you, Heidi? Is it just that Richardson woman driving you crazy, or is something else wrong?"

At the mention of Mrs. Richardson, Heidi remembered that, on top of everything else, her parents would be getting a phone call from the teacher that night.

"Um, Mrs. Richardson is mad at me, too." As briefly as possible, Heidi explained to her father about the Stoneheart poster.

"You don't give up, do you?" Matt asked, shaking his head.

"Yes, I do. In fact, I've given up. As of ten minutes ago." In a burst the rest of the story poured out, the terrible fight with Lynette and how Heidi had decided never to try to change anything ever again.

Matt pulled into an empty parking space in front of the Good Will building. He switched off the ignition, but made no move to get out of the car. "So it's all or nothing with you, Heidi, is that it? You'll do it your way or not at all?"

Heidi didn't understand what he was driving at.

"Look at me." Matt put a finger under Heidi's chin and lifted her face so that her eyes had to meet his. "There's nothing wrong with trying to change the world. But you come on like gangbusters, kiddo. Your idea of changing the world is to march in and *make* it change. You think it'll change just because you tell it to. But people aren't like that. You can't get them to change by posting a list of rules on the refrigerator that say, 'Hey, you, *change*!' Before you can change other people, you have to understand them. Try to look at things from their point of view, listen to where *they're* coming from. Why don't you make things a little easier for yourself and everyone else by working *with* the world once in a while, instead of *against* it? You might be surprised at the results."

"But I tried so hard!"

"I know you did. But I think all along you've been putting the cart before the horse. You were knocking yourself out to figure out *how* to change your teacher, Lynette, your mother and me. I'm saying that maybe you should have tried to answer some *why* questions first. Why is Mrs. Richardson so darn bent on cartridge pens? Why can't Lynette talk to her mother? Why don't your mother and I put the same premium on neatness that you do? If you started with the why questions, you might find that the how questions more or less answer themselves."

Heidi had to admit that what he said made some sense.

"And sometimes, Heidi, you're going to find that the world doesn't really need to change. Sometimes—perish the thought!—*you* may be the one who's in need of changing. End of lecture. Come on, let's go get those lawn mowers before Good Will realizes the treasures they're giving back to us."

Even though Heidi was relieved to spot her cartons

on the back of the Good Will truck, it was still depressing to be loading the same junk and clutter into Matt's car. Ahlenslager trash was turning out to be a great big boomerang, thrown away only to return right back home again.

"So why *do* you and Mom need so much stuff?" Heidi asked, once both lawn mowers had been somehow maneuvered onto the back seat.

"That's the spirit. Okay, here's an example. The lawn mowers you couldn't wait to be rid of? I used one of them for a solid month last summer when our power mower was in the shop."

"But you have *three* of them."

Matt sighed. "I know, I know. Call it a collection, Heidi. Your friend Lynette collects stuffed animals, I collect lawn mowers. I *like* lawn mowers. At worst it's a harmless eccentricity. And your mother's shoes, I swear she wears every darn pair she owns. You're not going to be wearing sneakers all your life, kiddo. When you're a world-famous accountant, believe me, you'll own quite an inventory of shoes yourself."

Heidi still had one last question. "But why does your stuff have to be all over the place?"

"You've got me there. I guess all I can say is that people have different temperaments. Some are messy, some are neat, and it can be tough when both kinds try to live in the same family. Let's see. Maybe we could work out a family strategy that would make neatness come easier for everyone. We could set aside one room of the house for mess, and then we could all try to get into the habit of tossing miscellaneous items in the Mess Room whenever a tidying fit was upon us."

"The Mess Room would fill up really fast," Heidi said doubtfully. "Before you know it, we'd need to have two Mess Rooms, then three. . . ."

"The other side of all this, Heidi, is for you to learn to be more tolerant. *Live and let live* strikes me as a more promising family motto than *A place for everything and everything in its place.* Your mother and I are pretty easygoing with you. You might try being more easygoing with us."

"I think the Mess Room sounds like a good idea," Heidi said quickly.

"We'll give it a try," her father said. "And maybe we can take the Ahlenslager House Rules down from the refrigerator?"

"Consider it done," Heidi promised.

━━━

After dinner, Heidi went upstairs to her room and climbed into her bed again. Even though everything had been made right with her parents, the rest of her life was still as wrong as could be. Any minute Mrs. Richardson would call, reminding Heidi of the stunning failure of Project Meanness. And the most painful memory of all stubbornly refused to go away: the look on Lynette's face when she realized that Heidi had taken it upon herself to divulge her guilty secret.

You're not my friend and you never were and you never will be. If only she had the day back to live over again. She would do so many things differently.

It must have been a terrible shock for Lynette to come home from her piano lesson and find Heidi there, in conference with her mother. And with or without Heidi's interference, Mrs. Lambert would have found out the truth, anyway. Lynette's crazy schemes for concealment had just about zero chance of success. What Heidi should have done was talk to Lynette honestly and straightforwardly, the way she would have wanted Lynette, in the same situation, to talk to her. Maybe she could have worked things out so that she and Lynette went to talk to her mother together, instead of H. P. Ahlenslager rushing off on a one-girl rescue mission.

In any case, it was too late now. What she had done could never be undone. But it wasn't too late to apologize. At least she could tell Lynette that she hadn't meant to barge in and take over her life. Or, rather, that was just what she had meant to do, but she was sorry for it now.

Slowly, Heidi made herself walk to the kitchen phone and dial Lynette's number.

Lynette answered on the second ring.

"Lynette, it's Heidi. I just wanted to say that—"

"Oh, Heidi, I'm sorry I got so mad before."

"*You're* sorry?"

"Yes, because my mom and I talked for a whole hour after you left. It was wonderful."

"But she sounded so mad."

"She was! But only because I hadn't come to talk to her myself about my problems. That's the part she was maddest about, that I had tried to hide everything from her. She was mad at herself, too. She kept asking me why, and I told her, you know, that I thought she had enough problems at work and everything, and I didn't want to make any more problems for her. And she said, 'But I'm your mother. If you have problems, I should know. That's what a mother is for.' She said she's going to try to organize some things differently so she's not so frazzled all the time, so she has more time just to listen. Can you believe it?"

"So you don't hate me?"

"No!"

"Because, you see, afterward I thought how much better it would have been if I had talked you into having us both go to your mother together. So you wouldn't have thought I was ratting on you behind your back. But it's like how I always think of something to invent after it's already been invented. I guess it's easier to think of what you should have done after you've gone and done something else. Has Mrs. Richardson called yet?"

"No, but it's funny, now that my parents know, I don't really care whether she calls or not. Anyway, my mom says she wants to talk to her. She says she and Mrs. Richardson should have had a talk a long time ago."

When they hung up, Heidi felt an enormous, crushing burden lifted from her heart. She and Lynette were friends again! She almost rushed downstairs for a big, celebratory bowl of chocolate ice cream. But there was still one last unresolved question of the day: What could she—what could anyone—do about Mrs. Richardson?

Well, for one, she *could* give up. Mrs. Oberlin was a pretty wise person, and she had said that Mrs. Richardson wasn't going to change. *She's not going to adapt to you; you're going to have to adapt to her.* Certainly everything Heidi had tried so far had failed, with the Stoneheart poster the biggest failure of all. But, for better or worse, H. P. Ahlenslager wasn't a giver-upper any more than Thomas Alva Edison had been. If there was a way to get Mrs. Richardson to change, Heidi was going to find it.

She tried to remember what her father had said, something about working with the world instead of against it. And that she couldn't change other people without making an effort first to understand them. Heidi knew all too well now that she couldn't march into Room 5C and *make* Mrs. Richardson change. But maybe she could start by thinking about why Mrs. Richardson was the way she was—for starters, why she cared so much about the cartridge pens.

Mrs. Richardson said that cartridge pens promoted self-discipline. They helped students approach their work in a careful, professional way. Okay. What if the students of Room 5C showed Mrs. Richardson that they were so self-disciplined that they didn't need cartridge pens? Or that there were other, better ways of developing self-discipline than making everybody write with the same leaky, awful pens? If Heidi could make her case persuasively enough, maybe Mrs. Richardson would listen. It couldn't turn out any worse than her other failed plans.

What if Heidi asked Mrs. Richardson if they could start a class newspaper? A newspaper required a lot of discipline, lots of planning and coordination and cooperation with others. Even Heidi's mother, who kept a sloppy checkbook and left her shoes all over the house, was fanatically painstaking and careful in her newspaper work. The paper could have articles on school events and soccer games and special things that happened to people. There would be book reports and a humor column by Skip and David and maybe a column on interesting inventions by H. P. Ahlenslager. Except that H. P. Ahlenslager, as editor of the *Room 5C Gazette*, would be too busy writing the paper's editorials. And the first editorial would explain why students who were disciplined enough to run their own newspaper hardly needed cartridge pens. Heidi could see the headline already: "Cartridge Pens or Pencils: We Want Freedom of Choice!"

The plan was so perfect that it took Heidi's breath away. Far better than an exposé by somebody's mother in the *Herald* would be a powerfully argued editorial in the students' own *Room 5C Gazette*. Mrs. Richardson was sure to let them do it because newspapers were so educational and promoted self-discipline a hundred times more than any pen could.

It might work! It just might possibly work!

TWELVE

Three weeks later the first issue of the *Room 5C Gazette* was about to go to press, Pam Sorenson and Heidi Ahlenslager, co-editors.

It had been Heidi's idea to ask Pam to share the editing honors. Pam was a hard worker, and the other students, understandably wary of Heidi's schemes, were more likely to cooperate with Pam at the helm of the new enterprise. So the two girls had gone together to ask Mrs. Richardson if they could have a newspaper as part of their unit in language arts. Mrs. Richardson had taken a day to think it over and then grudgingly said yes.

Now, with the contents of the first issue spread out in front of her in the computer lab, Heidi understood why her mother loved her work at the *Herald* so much. She could hardly wait to see copy after copy of their creation roll off the mimeograph machine, ready for the whole world to read, or at least all the fifth graders of Room 5C.

Carefully, she began typing the completed articles into one of the computers available for student use in the media center. Heidi was a poor typist, but on the computer it hardly mattered, since it was so easy to make corrections. In twenty minutes she had finished typing an article on the school soccer meet and Skip and David's roundup of the ten all-time dumbest elephant jokes. ("Why is an elephant like a grape?" "They're both purple, except for the elephant!")

Pam, working at the adjacent computer station, tapped Heidi on the shoulder. "I'm almost done with mine. How about you?"

"All I have left is Lynette's review of *The Pirates of Penzance* and my editorial."

"You're still going through with it? You know Mrs. Richardson has to approve the whole thing before we can start mimeographing."

Of course she was still going through with it. The editorial had been the reason for the newspaper in the first place.

"A newspaper has to have editorials."

"Yes, but we already have mine, about how students should behave better and be more courteous to the opposing team at soccer games."

"If there are two editors, there should be two editorials," Heidi insisted. "Don't worry, we're signing them, so she'll know which one is which." As if there could be any doubt.

Heidi turned back to her typing. The lunch period would be over in ten more minutes, and she and Pam would have to go back to class.

There! She was done at last. Tingling with anticipation, Heidi read over her editorial one last time on the computer screen.

CARTRIDGE PENS OR PENCILS:
WE WANT FREEDOM OF CHOICE!

One interesting fact about people is that they like different kinds of pens and pencils. Some like number 2 pencils, some like colored pencils, some like ballpoint pens, some like felt-tipped pens, some like cartridge pens. There is no one kind of pen or pencil that is best for everyone. Every person should have the right to choose his or her own kind.

One argument for using cartridge pens is that they develop self-discipline. But self-discipline can be developed in many other ways. For example, it takes self-discipline to run a newspaper. Everybody has to work together and plan ahead so that the issue comes out on time. People who are disciplined enough to have their own newspaper are disciplined enough to choose their own pens.

America is a free country. We have freedom of speech, freedom of press, and freedom of worship. We should also have freedom of pens. The students of Room 5C say: Give us liberty of pens, or give us death!

Heidi had borrowed the last line, in a slightly altered form, from the great patriot Patrick Henry, but she thought he wouldn't mind. She saved her work on the computer and clicked it off. If her edi-

119

torial didn't convince Mrs. Richardson, nothing on earth ever would.

The next day Heidi and Pam did the final layout for the six-page issue. Mrs. Sibley, who helped in the computer lab, showed them how to arrange the articles in two columns on the computer screen. Once Mrs. Richardson gave her approval, they could turn their six sheets of computer printout into mimeograph masters for mass production.

Mrs. Richardson was to take her copy of the *Room 5C Gazette* home with her to read that night. As soon as Heidi surrendered the newspaper into her hands, she began to have second thoughts about her editorial. It had seemed so fiery and eloquent when she had read it over to herself. But when she imagined Mrs. Richardson reading it, it began to seem less guaranteed to produce change.

At Heidi's house after school, Lynette tried to reassure her as they munched on potato chips and more of Lynette's now-famous Lipton onion soup dip.

"Look at it this way," Lynette suggested. "What's the worst that can happen if it makes Richardson mad?"

"If it makes her really mad?"

"Really mad."

"Well, then, I guess the worst that could happen would be that I'd be expelled."

All evening long, whenever the phone rang, Heidi

expected it to be Mrs. Richardson, calling in rage. But it never was. Heidi's father told her that she'd turn gray overnight if she didn't stop pacing and fretting.

Heidi had hoped that Mrs. Richardson would give them her reaction to the issue the first thing the next morning. But spelling followed math, and social studies followed spelling without a word. Finally, as the bell rang for lunch, Pam, emboldened by a look from Heidi, made her way to Mrs. Richardson's desk. Heidi held her breath.

"Um, Mrs. Richardson, did you have a chance to read our newspaper last night?"

"I read it."

"Um, is it all right?"

"It's fine."

Heidi could hardly believe her ears. "The whole thing is fine?" she asked.

"Yes, Heidi," Mrs. Richardson snapped. "I'm not in the habit of saying what I don't mean. You girls can ask Mrs. Sibley to help you with the printing now."

Delighted, Heidi made a dash for the door, but Mrs. Richardson called her back.

"Go ahead, Pam. Heidi, I'd like to talk to you for a minute."

When they were alone, Mrs. Richardson motioned Heidi to come up to her desk. Heidi steeled herself for the moment of truth. *The newspaper is fine, but you, Heidi Ahlenslager, are hereby expelled from Hazlewood School.*

"What I'm going to say should please you, Heidi. I've given careful thought to your editorial, and I think you made some valid points. Therefore I've decided to relax the cartridge pen requirement."

Heidi could hardly believe her ears. She wanted to race outside, to broadcast the glorious news to all the world, but she could tell that Mrs. Richardson wasn't through.

"I'm hoping now that we can put this behind us, Heidi, and get on with the rest of fifth grade. I'd like to see you take some of the energy you've directed toward fighting me and put it to other uses. I'm never going to be your favorite teacher, and I think you know that I don't particularly care. But I do care if a student of your academic abilities squanders her talents in classroom protests.

"There's a special math workshop for fifth and sixth graders offered for the first time this year by the state university. It's open to gifted students throughout the region who qualify for it on the basis of an examination. I'd like to help you prepare for that exam. It will be a lot of extra work for both of us, but I think it'll be worth it. What do you say, Heidi? Would you like the chance to move into a more advanced math program?"

"Yes," Heidi managed to say. "I'd like it a lot."

To do math—and to do math using a number 2 pencil—was Heidi's idea of heaven on earth.

"All right, then."

Heidi understood that she was dismissed. She felt like turning a cartwheel or two, but she didn't know how, and, besides, it would be undignified. Instead, only her heart was dancing as she made her way down to the all-purpose room to join Lynette and the others for lunch.

Walking home together after school, Heidi told Lynette everything.

"You're going to spend extra time with Mrs. Richardson? I'm sure glad I'm not you."

"She's not so bad." Actually, right then Heidi thought Mrs. Richardson was pretty wonderful. "I mean, she really does care, in her own way. You understand math better this year than you ever did with Miss Bellini. Right?"

"I got a ninety on the last quiz, the one on percentages," Lynette admitted. "But I still think she's mean."

"Okay, sometimes, but you can't let it get to you."

"Everything gets to me," Lynette said. "The day my parents and I had our big talk about Mrs. Richardson, they said I'm too sensitive."

"My father said I need to be *more* sensitive. You know, like to other people. Like to Mrs. Richardson. But I have an idea. Let's have a secret signal, and any time Mrs. Richardson says something mean or sarcastic to you, I'll turn around and make the secret sign, and it'll make her meanness into a game, sort of."

"What kind of sign?"

"I'll stick out my tongue twice, real fast, like this." Heidi poked out her tongue twice in rapid succession.

"What if Mrs. Richardson sees you and asks what you're doing?"

"I'll say, 'This is the secret signal I give my friend Lynette whenever you've been mean to her.'"

"You wouldn't!"

"I would," said H. P. Ahlenslager calmly. Then again, maybe she wouldn't. She really wanted to try working with Mrs. Richardson, instead of against her.

She and Lynette reached home. Once inside, Heidi gazed at the cluttered living room with mingled despair and resignation.

"Tell me honestly, Lynette. Do you think this house looks any neater since we started having the Mess Room?"

"Honestly? No. But, Heidi, I love your house the way it is, and I love your parents the way they are."

"So do I," Heidi said, and it was true.

The girls fixed themselves platefuls of Aunt Jemima's toaster waffles, with butter and syrup. Then, picking their way across rooms strewn with shoes and piles of pharmaceutical journals, they retreated into Heidi's room, a sanctuary of order and cleanliness, where there was a place for everything and everything in its place. Lynette put Gilbert and Sullivan's *Mikado* on Heidi's little record player, and the music made Heidi so happy she picked up her math book and hugged it.

"When does the next issue of the *Room 5C Gazette* come out?" Lynette asked.

"Soon. Very soon." And H. P. Ahlenslager, world-famous accountant, mathematician, map-maker, inventor, and newspaper editor, reached for a freshly sharpened number 2 pencil, ready for anything.

Other Avon Camelot Books by
Claudia Mills

CLAUDIA MILLS is a popular author of books for young people. Her novels include the Avon Camelot book, *Cally's Enterprise*. Ms. Mills is also the editor at the Center for Philosophy and Public Policy at the University of Maryland. She lives with her husband and son in Takoma Park, Maryland.